SKRUJ

HOLIDATE WITH AN ALIEN

HONEY PHILLIPS

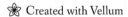 Created with Vellum

CHAPTER 1

"*H*e did *what?*"

Although Skruj did not raise his voice, the Zyran legal representative who had delivered the unwelcome news took a step back from the desk, his tail lashing nervously.

"He, err, added a codicil to his will shortly before he died."

"He never mentioned it to me."

"I understand you did not, err, see him often during his last illness."

Was there a hint of disapproval in the male's voice, despite his outward deference? Perhaps—the Zyrans valued their complicated hierarchy of relationships—but the opinions of others had ceased to matter to him long ago.

"I have been busy running our business—the business for which I was supposed to receive his shares after his passing."

"And you still will, as long as you comply with the provisions in the codicil," the little male said eagerly. "It's only a few very simple conditions."

"Which are?"

His voice was even colder, and the male shrank back a little more.

"There are three, err, social events that you must attend—for at least an hour each time—and a document to review."

Social events? Documents? His deceased partner had obviously completely lost his mental faculties during the last stage of his illness. Perhaps he should have visited him after all, but at the time he hadn't seen any profit in taking the time to do so. He'd already taken control of the aspects of the business Jakoba had previously managed.

"Is that the codicil?" he asked, gesturing to the documents the Zyran was clutching.

"Yes, Master Skruj."

"Give it to me and then leave."

The male's tail lashed again.

"I am required to make sure you—"

He held out his hand, claws flexing.

"Now."

The Zyran gulped and handed them over, but he remained hovering across from Skruj's desk. Was the male incapable of understanding a simple order?

"Leave," he growled, and the male finally fled his office, leaving him in peace to examine the infernal codicil.

How could Jakoba have done this to him? Neither of them had any family—nor any interest in acquiring one—and they had made the wills when they agreed to go into business together. The partnership had been mutually beneficial, combining his banking assets with Jakoba's shipping and import business. The two males had never been friends, but they had a mutual interest in increasing their profits. He'd never considered the possibility of his former partner amending the terms of their agreement.

I should have known better than to rely on the word of another.

Frowning, he picked up the document and read through it. It was exactly as the Zyran had described—three specific events that would be occurring over the next month as part of the Londrian holiday season.

Holiday season. *Bah.* He hated this time of year. The vast majority of his employees considered it an excuse for short hours and lax behavior. They even expected to take paid time away from their positions. He had been forced to provide them with the First Day holiday, but he had drawn the line at any additional time.

He examined the list of events again. They began with the annual reunion at Zenith Academy. His mouth tightened at the thought. His memories of his time at the elite boarding school were... unpleasant. Although he had the satisfaction of knowing that he could buy or sell most of his previous classmates, he intensely disliked the thought of an hour in their company.

The tickets to the event were included with the papers. At least the bastard hadn't made him pay for them. *Tickets*—why were there two tickets? He picked up the codicil again and read through the provisions at the beginning of the list.

Companion. He was required to take a companion.

What the hell had Jakoba been thinking? He didn't have a companion and had no desire for one, not since... He shoved the thought away and scowled down at the document, considering the wording of the codicil.

He pressed the button to call his secretary, Miggs.

"Has the Zyran left the building?"

"I... I'm not sure, Master Skruj."

"Well, find out," he said impatiently. Why couldn't he find an employee capable of thinking for himself?

"Y-yes, sir."

After far too long a wait, Miggs came back on the line.

"He's here, Master Skruj. Should I send him in?" he asked breathlessly.

"Did I say I wanted to see him? No. Just ask him if the companion is truly a requirement."

There was a moment of astonished silence.

"Companion, Master Skruj?"

"Must I repeat every question?"

The chill in his voice made the fool stutter.

"No, sir. Of course not, sir."

Another moment of silence.

"Master Rolas says that he is afraid so. Would you like him—"

He closed the channel.

Damn, damn, damn. Where the hell was he going to find someone to fill that role? One of his employees, perhaps? He tried to remember if he had any female employees who might be suitable. There weren't many in his immediate employ—they had an unfortunate tendency to burst into tears at the simplest request—and none of the ones he could remember were even remotely suitable.

If he must take a companion, it would have to be someone suitable to his level of wealth. Which meant... hiring someone. An expense he did not wish to make, but he supposed it would be worth it to satisfy this ridiculous condition. And less expensive than hiring a legal representative to argue against it in court. He scowled and picked up his communicator.

H<small>E</small> <small>WAS STILL SCOWLING A WEEK LATER WHEN</small> L<small>ITTIMA</small>, his steward, escorted the latest disastrous candidate for the companionship role out of the room. Not only had the female been unattractive and ill bred, she had been foolish enough to believe that he was interested in hiring her for a physical relationship. She'd actually gone as far as placing her hand over his genitals before he was able to disengage her and order Littima to remove her.

Perhaps he should have hired the employment agency after all, but at the time he'd balked at paying for what was surely a simple request and decided to handle it himself. Unfortunately, none of the few candidates who had answered his advertisement were remotely suitable. Now he had less than three days left and the employment agency would no doubt want to charge him an additional outrageous fee because of the abbreviated timeframe.

He had just placed his hand reluctantly on the communication panel when Littima reentered.

"Yes?" he demanded impatiently.

"There is another applicant, Master Skruj." Littima had an odd expression on his usually neutral face.

"Is she suitable?"

"She is an attractive female..."

"But?"

"She is human, sir."

Human? Londria was one of the planetary systems that had agreed to take in refugees from that dying planet, but he'd had little contact with any of them. Still, the presence of an exotic female at his side might work. She would have no family connections to trouble him, and no doubt as a refugee she wouldn't expect much payment for her services. The last thought decided him.

"Send her in."

Littima bowed his head and left, returning a moment later with a small human female. Too small. He would have preferred a taller female, but then again, her diminutive size would make him look more powerful in comparison. Her skin did not have the markings all Londrians bore, but it was a pleasant creamy color. Her rather untidy hair was a dark golden color that was not unattractive and her features were regular enough, but her body was concealed by a pink coat that looked far too light for the current temperatures.

"Take off your coat."

She'd been looking around his study but when he spoke, she jumped and then looked at him directly. Green eyes, as green as the forests outside the town where he was born. A faint, unwelcome shock of what felt like recognition hit him as their eyes met. Annoyed, he repeated the order more harshly.

"Take off your clothing."

CHAPTER 2

"What did you say?"

Bobbi forced her attention from her surroundings to the huge Londrian sitting behind the big desk that was the only piece of furniture in the dark wood-paneled room. He was wearing a severe dark suit, but the tailored lines did nothing to conceal his powerful body. The irregular pattern of golden lines typical for a Londrian formed a striking contrast to his dark charcoal skin. He had a hard face with sharp, angular features but a surprisingly sensual mouth.

Her gaze threatened to linger there and she quickly dragged it away. As she did, their eyes met and it felt as if all the breath left her body. His eyes were golden too, as bright as burning embers, and she felt an answering wave of heat before she shook her head and forced herself to concentrate on the conversation.

"I have absolutely no intention of removing my clothing. The advertisement said that this was a strictly social position. If you had something else in mind, I'll just leave—"

"I assure you I have no interest in anything of that nature." The cold voice practically dripped with disdain. "I want you to remove your coat so I can judge how you will look in Londrian dress. If you are to accompany me, you will need to be suitably dressed."

As much as she hated to comply, it wasn't an unreasonable request under the circumstances. She sighed and began unbuttoning her coat as he waited impatiently. Despite his denial, there was something unexpectedly erotic about removing her clothing under that hot, golden gaze, and by the time she slipped off her coat her cheeks were burning. Her blush deepened as his gaze drifted down over her body.

She was appropriately dressed in a typical Londrian outfit—a long floating tunic over narrow pants, belted at the waist. The clothes were far from new but they were clean and neatly pressed, and she lifted her chin to return his gaze when it finally drifted back up to her face.

"Well?"

"You are not very tall."

Despite the disapproving note in his voice, her sense of humor got the better of her.

"You didn't need me to remove my coat to know that," she said dryly. "And I'm not going to grow anymore, so if height is a requirement..."

"It is not. It's unfortunate, but not unacceptable."

She barely managed to keep from rolling her eyes. She really could use the income from this job.

"Other than my lack of inches, are there any other faults?"

His eyes ran back down over her body and the tips of her breasts suddenly tingled. Praying that he couldn't see her nipples stiffen, she arched a brow and waited.

"No," he said at last. "The rest of you is acceptable."

"Gee, thanks," she muttered under her breath.

"What is your name?" he continued.

"I'm Roberta Cratchar, but everyone calls me Bobbi. What's your name? All your servant said was Master Skruj."

"That is my name."

"You don't have another name?"

"Not one which I care to use." He frowned at her. "I had not anticipated that a human would respond to my advertisement."

"Is that a problem?"

He hesitated for an endless moment as she held her breath and prayed, then finally shook his head.

"No. It may even be an advantage. Any slips you make will be put down to the fact that you are a newcomer to Londria."

The condescension in his voice, let alone his assumption that she would make mistakes, annoyed her, but she managed to paste a smile on her face.

"Are there any other requirements?"

"You seem capable of carrying on a brief conversation if pressed, although I doubt anyone will speak to you."

Could he be more arrogant? She choked down the impulse to tell him where to stuff his job and smiled again.

"Can you tell me more about the job? I understand it involves three social events?"

He scowled down at his desk before giving an abrupt nod. His anger brought life to those cold features, rendering them somehow more attractive. Not that she was interested, of course.

"Yes. You will accompany me to each one and act as if you are my regular companion. An hour at each event will suffice, plus the time required to travel back and forth."

"Back and forth here to your house?"

"Of course. Why?"

She sighed. "Public transportation doesn't serve your neighborhood, and private transportation is too expensive for the amount you are offering."

Even public transportation across the city would cut into her earnings.

He tapped his fingers on the desk. They made an odd clicking noise, and she suddenly noticed his claws. They looked awfully dark and dangerous...

She was still staring at them when he nodded again.

"My vehicle will transport you to your home after each assignment. That will be the most cost effective option."

"To and from," she said firmly, holding her breath. To her delight, he gave a reluctant assent and she smiled at him.

"Thank you. And the clothing? You said Londrian formal dress."

"You don't possess any?"

This time she couldn't stop herself from rolling her eyes.

"No, my social calendar isn't exactly full of formal events."

"Social calendar?" His eyes flickered over her again. "You will not be seen in public with another male during this period. While it is unlikely you would be noticed, it would be... unfortunate if you were."

Since she couldn't even remember the last time she'd been on a date, that wouldn't be difficult.

"That's fine."

"You will also be required to sign a document agreeing not to discuss any aspect of our arrangement with anyone else. That is, I assume you can write?"

"Of course I can write! I'm not stupid."

She glared at him, and he actually looked a little startled.

"I was simply asking if you could write Londrian."

I need this job. She took a deep breath and forced herself to nod.

"Yes. We were taught on the transport trip once our destination had been determined."

"Very well. Do you have any other questions?"

13

"Since I don't have any formal clothes, what do you want to do about clothing?"

"You will require a different outfit for each event." That sensuous mouth twisted as if he'd eaten something sour. "I will provide funds to purchase the clothing, along with instructions as to the appropriate attire."

Since she wasn't familiar with formal clothing, this time his assumption of her ignorance was easier to swallow. She nodded, then gave him a curious look.

"Why are you even doing this? Surely someone of your... importance has many companions from which to choose."

The golden eyes burned down at her, and her breath caught again.

"My reasons are not your concern."

Fair enough. She had no intention of telling him why she was taking the job either.

"I understand."

From his expression he disagreed, but all he did was pull out a data pad.

"This contains the terms of the contract, as well as the non-disclosure agreement. Read through it and sign it."

"Please," she automatically added, the same way she could have corrected her brother. Timmy would have understood; Skruj clearly did not.

"Please what?"

"Nothing." She reached out to take the datapad. "I want to read through this."

14

"Of course."

Despite his agreement, he did not offer her a seat and sat watching her as she read, those dark claws tapping impatiently on the desk.

"This specifies a quarter of the payment after each of the first two events, with half being reserved until after the final event. Why not even thirds?"

"To ensure that you complete the assignment."

"I suppose that makes sense," she agreed reluctantly. She could really have used the credits sooner, but she'd make it work.

Taking a deep breath, she signed the documents, then handed the tablet back. "I would like a printed copy."

He raised an eyebrow, looking almost... impressed? Then he nodded and pressed a few buttons.

"My steward will provide it for you when you leave. The first event is two nights from now. I will send my vehicle for you at nineteen hundred hours. Provide my steward with your address."

He reached into a drawer and pulled out a small golden credit chit and offered it to her.

"You may use this to purchase your first outfit."

As she reached for it their hands touched, sending an almost electric shock through her body. *It's just because his hand is cold*, she told herself even though she had that odd breathless feeling again. His hand flexed against hers before he quickly drew it back.

"You may go," he said, his voice harsh.

"Wait a minute. Shouldn't we at least have a conversation first? You said I was supposed to be your regular companion but no one is going to believe that unless I know something about you."

He had already pulled up a monitor and keyboard and didn't bother to look over at her.

"Littima will provide an information packet along with a copy of the contract."

She doubted that such a document would be sufficient to explain this cold, reserved male, but she decided not to press him.

"Fine. I'm looking forward to our date," she added impishly.

That brought his head around, eyes blazing.

"It is not a date. It is a job."

"I know that and you know that, but it will be a lot easier to convince other people if you act like it's a date. Might as well start now."

That surprisingly attractive scowl crossed his face before he gave a reluctant nod.

"I look forward to seeing you again."

Since the sour lemon look was back on his face, the statement was remarkably unconvincing, but she gave him her sweetest smile.

"I can hardly wait, snookums."

Then she fled before he had a chance to respond.

CHAPTER 3

T hree hundred credits!

Bobbi clutched the documents Littima had given her to her chest as the door to Skruj's mansion closed behind her. She couldn't believe she'd gotten the job. When she'd seen the advertisement, she'd been extremely skeptical, but she had desperately needed the extra income.

Although she worked full time at a clothing factory, the job only paid enough to keep a roof over their heads and food on the table—it didn't stretch to luxuries. She'd often thought of trying to find something else, but her shift matched the hours that Timmy was in school. And if he had one of his all too frequent sick days, they had provided her with a portable sewing machine so she could work from home. Not many jobs would be as flexible.

But it was the lack of anything extra that had driven her to answer the advertisement. She was determined to make this a special holiday for her little brother Timmy, no matter what it took. And now she would have enough credits to give him the kind of Christmas he deserved.

The kind of Christmas she'd had before her mom got sick and her dad started drinking and the population of Earth found out that the sun was going to destroy their planet and their only hope of a future was traveling for years to some alien planet... A planet her mom hadn't lived long enough to see.

Blinking back the familiar wash of pain, she concentrated on the present. Time to get back home. Shivering, she pulled the collar of her coat tighter around her neck as she set off. It was a light spring coat, not intended for the type of chill that had been creeping over Londria for the past few weeks, but it was the only one she had. For that matter, it had barely been enough inside the cold rooms of his mansion.

At least inside she'd been protected from the breeze that had started to pick up as the early winter dusk crept over the street. Thank goodness it was only a breeze. It wasn't cold enough for snow, and the wide street was dry and clear—and dark.

Uneasy about the gathering darkness, she glanced down at the old-fashioned watch that had belonged to her mother and sighed. It was going to be fully dark soon, and although the stately townhouses lining the street were impressive, they were not exactly overflowing with life and activity. At least most of them had some concession to the holiday season—bushes outlined in tasteful white lights or white candles in the windows—unlike Skruj's house. The tall residence behind her not only lacked any decorations, the only lights showing were the porch light flickering next to the door and a faint, dim glow coming from an upstairs room.

What a strange male, she thought as she increased her pace, her heels tapping briskly on the pavement. Strange but not... unattractive, especially when emotion brought life to that stern face. *Not that it matters.* Her job was simply to act like his girlfriend and his looks were irrelevant.

Not that she was exactly sure how a Londrian female was supposed to act towards her date in public. Several of her friends at the factory were Londrian but the factory wasn't the kind of place where you shared intimate details of your love life. Although the thought of Skruj having a love life seemed ridiculous, let alone dating.

Her mind wandered, imagining him holding hands, exchanging kisses. Would the hard planes of his face soften with affection? A faint quiver of what she refused to admit was arousal tightened her nipples, and she shook her head impatiently. *Stop it, Bobbi.* Just because she hadn't had a boyfriend in a long time didn't mean she had to fantasize about someone who would never have looked at her under normal circumstances. She wondered again why a clearly rich, attractive male was reduced to hiring a companion.

Maybe he's trying to divert attention from a secret love affair, she thought, then rolled her eyes. He didn't seem like the type who would care enough about other people's opinions to try and hide anything. *Or maybe he's some kind of secret agent.*

She amused herself with ever more outrageous theories until she finally left the residential area behind and joined the crowds thronging a main avenue. Although Londrians predominated, a wide variety of species surrounded her—a group of Zyrans chatting with an alien with tentacles for hair, a human with a child of a race she couldn't identify, a blue-skinned male followed by two gawking females, and even a floating glass bubble containing what looked like a jellyfish bobbed merrily along the sidewalk.

The buildings were equally varied, ranging from towering skyscrapers to old buildings repurposed into boutiques and restaurants, and she found herself smiling. She loved the energy of the city and under other circumstances would have taken the opportunity simply to walk and watch, but she'd been gone long enough. A hover cab floated by, and for a moment she was tempted to hail it—the journey back across town would be long and tedious—but the money was for Timmy's Christmas and she didn't want to waste a penny of it.

Forty minutes, two bus rides, and one subway trip later, she wearily climbed the steps to the boarding house where they lived. The life of the city wasn't quite so appealing when you were crammed in with half of it on the subway or struggling to get on a bus. Her spirits revived when she stepped inside and took a deep breath. Whatever Mrs. M'gid was cooking smelled delicious.

Her landlady opened the door before she had a chance to knock and stepped out into the hallway. Mrs. M'gid was Coomar—a race native to one of the other planets in this system. The short blue fur covering her sturdy body was ruffled, but her smile was as warm as always.

"Is everything all right? How's Timmy?" Bobbi asked anxiously.

"He's just fine, dear. He's been telling stories to Kami to keep her out from under my feet while I'm cooking. Such a sweet boy."

He really was—endlessly patient with the numerous M'gid children, and with his own limitations.

"How did things go this afternoon?"

"I got the job! Three evenings, just like the ad said, and he'll send a car to get me each time."

"That's wonderful." Mrs. M'gid beamed happily. "Who's your new employer?"

"It's a big secret so you can't tell anyone, but his name is Skruj."

Mrs. M'gid's eyes widened.

"Skruj? You don't mean the Miser of Parkan, do you?"

"Maybe? Big, dark skin marked with gold? Have you heard of him?"

"Oh, yes. He's famous, or perhaps I mean infamous. They say he clings to a credit so tightly that it shrieks for mercy. Mr. M'gid saw him at a civic meeting—where he flatly refused to donate any credits to the library fund. Can you imagine? And him as rich as Croton!"

"He did seem a little... conservative with his wealth," she said uncomfortably, remembering the minimal lights and the lack of heat.

Mrs. M'gid sniffed.

"I imagine he did. Are you sure he's going to pay you?"

She patted the pocket where she'd placed the documents. "I have a signed contract."

"I just hope that's enough," her landlady said gloomily before straightening her apron and smiling again. "Now come and have dinner with us. And don't bother arguing with me. I insist."

She had opened her mouth to do just that, but instead she laughed and gave Mrs. M'gid an impulsive hug.

"Thank you. You're so kind to us."

"We're all put into this world to look out for each other. Come along."

As usual, the cluttered apartment was loud and chaotic, the four M'gid children racing around and making enough noise for ten. No, three M'gid children. The fourth was still perched on Timmy's lap, sucking sleepily on her thumb.

"Hi, sis," Timmy said, smiling at her over Kami's head. "Did you have a good day?"

As usual, her throat tightened a little when she saw him. He looked so much like their mother. He had inherited her pale skin and dark hair, as well as her fragile health, whereas Bobbi took after their more robust father. Only their startlingly green eyes were the same—although his were often shadowed.

"I did, thanks. How are you feeling?"

"Much better. I think the medicine is working."

She didn't believe him, but she didn't press him, merely keeping a careful eye on him as they gathered at the M'gid table. He ate almost nothing, but Mrs. M'gid quietly handed him a cup of broth and he sipped on that as the others ate. Afterwards, they climbed the stairs to their small apartment and she tried—and failed—not to worry about how slowly he took the stairs.

"By the way, I'm going to be taking a couple of evening jobs," she told him once they were inside.

"You're taking a second job? But you already work such long hours."

"It's just three evenings, helping out at a few social events. It's the busy season. You don't mind, do you?"

She kept her voice deliberately casual, but he shot her a penetrating look.

"Of course I don't mind. You don't have to stay with me all the time. You could even go out just to have fun."

"I have more fun here. Now go get ready for bed."

He rolled her eyes at her but obeyed, and she breathed a sigh of relief. She'd been afraid he would ask more questions. She really didn't want to lie to him, but she didn't want him to worry either.

By the time he'd finished his routine and was tucked up in bed, he was obviously exhausted. She sat beside him until his eyelids closed and his breathing slowed. His face was too thin, his cheeks hollow, and her heart ached. The latest medicine clearly wasn't countering the effects of the disease that had attacked his system since birth. Perhaps an Earth doctor would have had a solution. On Londria, the doctors were baffled.

She was terrified she was going to lose him, but she refused to give up hope. And for now, she was determined to do everything she could to make this a joyous Christmas for him.

CHAPTER 4

*S*kruj frowned at his surroundings as Littima drove slowly down the crowded street. If he had known his... date lived in the slums, he would never have decided to accompany his steward to pick her up. *You didn't have to come,* a tiny voice in his head argued, but he ignored it. He had decided that there was a possibility that she was right—a *small* possibility—and it might be helpful to know a little bit about her before the reunion began.

Accompanying Littima would also be more cost effective since he would not be required to travel back across the city to pick him up.

Not slums, he amended reluctantly as he took a second look. Crowded and showing signs of delayed maintenance, but most of the buildings were clean and obviously cared for. Many of them were already displaying signs of the holiday season in bright and often clashing colors.

But despite those efforts the poverty of the area brought back unpleasant memories from long ago, and he was frowning when Littima came to a halt.

"This is the address, sir."

At one time the three-story townhouse had probably been a desirable residence. Now the paint was peeling, one of the windows was clearly cracked, and the roof sagged. The bright red paint on the door was obviously a vain attempt to detract from the general shabbiness. It didn't work.

"Well?" he demanded a moment later. "Aren't you going to get her?"

"It is customary for a male to meet his... companion at her door."

As always, Littima's voice was perfectly neutral but Skruj had known him long enough to detect the faintest hint of disapproval in the rigid set of his shoulders.

"She is an escort, not a companion," he said through gritted teeth. "There is no need to begin the pretense yet. Go and get her."

"Yes, sir."

But as Littima stepped out of the vehicle, the red door opened and Roberta appeared. She looked so different that it took him a full second to recognize her. The somewhat bedraggled waif had disappeared, replaced by an elegant female. She was wearing a long gown in a shade of green so dark it was almost black. The form-fitting garment followed the slender curves of her body down to her knees before widening into a fanciful froth of fabric that formed a slight train. More fabric was gathered at her shoulders above a square neckline that dipped slightly between her breasts.

She looked stunning. *Acceptable,* he reminded himself. That was all that was important.

Littima glanced at him, but when he made no attempt to leave the vehicle went to meet her at the bottom of the stairs.

"Good evening, Miss Roberta."

"Good evening, Littima. Please call me Bobbi. Is your knee feeling better tonight?"

"Quite, miss. Thank you for asking."

Littima was having problems with his knee? Why hadn't he mentioned it? Or had he? He usually dismissed any claim of illness as nothing more than an attempt to avoid work, but Littima had been with him a long time. He frowned, then reluctantly decided to inquire. Later.

His frown deepened as Roberta took Littima's arm and let him escort her to the vehicle. Hadn't he specified no other males? *I'm the one who sent him,* he reminded himself, but he still found the act... troubling for reasons he didn't care to examine.

"Brrr."

Roberta shivered dramatically as she finally climbed in next to him, bringing a rush of cold air and a subtle, intriguing scent, and he gave her a disapproving look.

"You should be wearing a cloak."

Her eyes flashed in a disturbingly appealing way as Littima took the wheel and the vehicle began to move.

"I'm sure I should, but I don't have a cloak or a coat to go with this outfit."

"You could have purchased one. What did you do with the rest of the credits?"

Her mouth dropped open.

"Are you insane? I didn't even think I was going to have enough to pay for a dress, but fortunately someone had returned this one and the shop was willing to let me have it at a discount."

"It is *used?*"

The knowledge brought back more unpleasant memories.

She picked at the skirt, suddenly looking uncomfortable.

"They said it had never been worn. Of course it didn't fit, but I raised the hem and took in the bodice—both of which took a considerable amount of time by the way."

The results were certainly impressive. The upper part of the dress clung to her body like a second skin, accentuating the subtle swell of her breasts above the low neckline... He shifted in his seat as his shaft stirred. Ridiculous.

"You appear to have done an adequate job."

"Gee, I'm overwhelmed by your praise."

She crossed her arms and glared at him, which only served to emphasize her breasts even more. He quickly looked away, focusing on the partition separating them from Littima.

"I suppose I could increase the clothing allowance next time. By a small amount," he added hastily. There was no need to get carried away. "How much for a cloak?"

"There was one in the shop for three hundred credits," she said, her voice suspiciously innocent, and he jerked his head back to look at her.

"Three hundred credits? That's outrageous."

She suddenly laughed, her face brightening.

"I know. Why, I could feed Timmy and I for a year on—" She broke off abruptly, then gave him a teasing look. "It makes me suspect that I am being underpaid."

"You are receiving a ridiculously large amount for three hours of work," he said stiffly.

"You're not including the travel time, plus the shopping time, and then the sewing time."

Perhaps she had a point, but they had made a deal.

"You agreed to the terms. Who is Timmy?" he added before she could argue with him. "We agreed to no males."

He hadn't liked the thought of another male before, and he liked it even less now with her slender body only inches away from him.

"He's my brother." Clearly not wanting to discuss the matter, she changed the subject. "Your information packet—which, by the way, was not at all informative—said you attended Zenith Academy?"

"Yes."

He didn't volunteer any additional information, and she sighed.

"So tell me about it. Not the information in the packet but what you might have told a... companion. What does it look like?

Where did you live? Did you have any friends we might meet tonight? Or teachers?"

"It is a very large complex with many large buildings, including the dormitory where I lived," he said dismissively. "And there is no one I care to discuss."

Her face softened and she put her hand on his arm.

"Don't you have any happy memories?"

He stared down at the small, pale fingers on his arm, the warmth of her touch branding his arm.

"Master Fezzer," he said, surprising himself. "He was our housemaster, and he was... kind."

Kind to an orphaned boy with too many brains and too little money. For a time he'd actually thought he might fit in at the school, but that illusion hadn't lasted.

She still hadn't removed her hand, but he did his best to ignore those delicate little fingers and the warmth radiating from that single point of contact.

"Enough of this fruitless discussion of my past. Is there anything I should know about you?"

"My brother and I arrived on the first transport ship two, no, three years ago. I still remember how strange it was to be on land again after five years on the transport ship." Her eyes gazed unseeingly into the distance, before she shook her head. "But your government was very helpful and we... adjusted. I managed to find a job at a clothing factory, and we moved into the boarding house. We were very lucky—Mrs. M'gid is wonderful."

There was a shadow in her eyes despite her smile, but he didn't pursue it. No one appreciated an attempt to pry their secrets out of them.

"You do not need to divulge any of that information, if anyone has the temerity to ask."

Her lips pursed in a way he refused to find endearing.

"Why not? I have nothing to be ashamed of."

"No, but as my... companion you would not be expected to work. Nor to live in such an area."

Her eyes flashed.

"I'd rather live there than on that cold, dark street where you live."

"It is the finest residential district in the city," he said stiffly. When he'd foreclosed on the previous owner, he'd been unable to resist taking possession of such a visible symbol of his new wealth.

"I suppose that depends on what you value."

"I assure you it has the highest property values—"

"I wasn't talking about money," she interrupted.

"It is the only objective standard."

"Sometimes subjective standards are more important."

Before he could counter her ridiculous argument, the vehicle slowed to pass through a set of tall iron gates. They had arrived.

CHAPTER 5

*B*obbi peered around eagerly as they passed through the gates. Although night had long since fallen, the grounds were tastefully illuminated with small concealed lights that highlighted the immaculate landscaping. Several of the gracious buildings lining the long drive were also illuminated— mellow stone buildings softened by ancient vines.

"What a beautiful place. You were lucky to go to school here."

"Yes."

His voice sounded odd, and she shot him a quick glance from under her lashes. Any hint of life she might have seen on his face during their journey had disappeared, replaced by a cold sneer. But his hand had clenched in a slight betraying gesture, his claws flexing. He clearly did not want to be here—but why? And why had he come anyway?

As the vehicle slowed to a crawl, she saw they were in a line of vehicles dropping off guests. Well-dressed, laughing people were walking down a long pathway beneath a canopy of vines woven with pretty, twinkling lights. An open canopy. She sighed. It was going to be a cold walk.

When it was their turn to be dropped off, Skruj surprised her by telling her to wait before coming around and opening her door himself. She took his hand, feeling the same spark of electricity as their skin touched, and did her best to ignore the cold. Apparently unsuccessfully because he frowned down at her as he placed her hand on his arm.

"You will be cold."

"I know. I feel like one of those silly teenagers who refuses to wear a coat so the boys can see her cute outfit."

"Is that why you didn't wear a sensible outer garment?" he asked, barely acknowledging the servant who rushed over to meet them before they headed down the path.

"Of course not. I already told you that I didn't have anything. Or did you want me to wear my pink coat?"

He frowned again, then to her utter shock paused long enough to unfasten his cloak and wrap it around her shoulders. Still warm from his body and smelling deliciously of his masculine scent, it settled around her like a warm embrace and she couldn't prevent a sigh of relief.

"Are you sure?"

"Yes. You will be of little use to me if you die of exposure."

Was that a joke? She could have sworn the corners of his mouth turned up for the briefest instant, but then he put her hand on his arm and started walking again.

"That's a female for you. They always hate to cover up their pretty gowns," a male voice said from behind them.

The tone was clearly jovial, and she glanced back over her shoulders to see a portly Londrian smiling at her. He could have been the same age as Skruj, with wide silver lines patterning his deep blue skin, but he had a friendly, jovial face. He winked at her.

"Don't mind me, my dear. I'm just a harmless old bachelor."

She smiled at him. "Hello. Are you here for the reunion as well?"

"Yes, and—" His eyes widened as Skruj sighed and turned around as well. "Eben? Eben, is that you?"

"I prefer Skruj."

The arm under her fingers was rigid with tension, but the other male appeared oblivious.

"Well, bless my buttons. I certainly didn't expect to see you here."

"You believed me unworthy, Chivi?"

"What?" The other male appeared genuinely confused. "I simply meant that you have never attended one of our reunions before. I'm delighted to see you."

When Skruj didn't respond, she stepped in.

"It's a pleasure to meet you. My name is Bobbi."

Chivi swept her a bow, wheezing a little as he straightened.

"Charmed. Have you visited the Academy before?"

"No, I'm afraid not. But the campus is very attractive."

Skruj made an impatient sound and tugged on her arm to get her moving again. Not to be deterred, Chivi fell into step next to them.

"They do their best to keep it that way." Chivi chuckled. "We never made it easy for them. Do you remember when old Fezzer had to rescue us from the head gardener after we kicked a ball through his prize flower bed, Eben?"

Chivi laughed again, apparently not bothered by Skruj's lack of response, and continued to regale her with tales of their adventures at the school. Some of the activities were new to her, but they all sounded perfectly normal—things she could see her brother doing if he were in better health. So why had Skruj been so reluctant to return?

He didn't respond to Chivi's ongoing conversation—which didn't seem to bother the other male at all—but he did occasionally nod, and his muscles were no longer quite so tense.

They finally came to the end of the long walkway and entered into a spacious foyer, filled with people talking and laughing and removing their outer garments. A uniformed servant hurried over to take her cloak, and she rather reluctantly let him take it. Having Skruj's cloak wrapped around her had been like having a protective arm across her shoulders. She felt more exposed in the fashionable dress, but Chivi gave a low whistle of appreciation.

"Positively charming. I can see why you were so reluctant to cover up that dress."

"The wearer is more attractive than the dress," Skruj snapped, startling both of them.

He thought she was attractive? She couldn't prevent a pleased smile even as Chivi bowed apologetically.

"Of course. I meant no insult, my dear."

"None taken." She tightened her grip on Skruj's arm when his lips parted and he thankfully remained silent. "What do we do now?"

"Eat, drink, and be merry, of course. They always put on a much too delectable buffet." Chivi rubbed his stomach regretfully and she laughed.

"The food was always... acceptable."

This time Skruj managed to keep his tone relatively polite, and she gave him an encouraging smile.

"There will be dancing later," Chivi added. "I would be delighted if you would honor me with a dance, my dear. That is, if you don't mind, Eben?"

Skruj clearly did not like the idea, but he didn't immediately snap at his friend. They were making progress.

"Perhaps," she said diplomatically. "I'm afraid I'm not very familiar with Londrian dances, although Eben is trying to teach me. Aren't you, snookums?"

Fortunately, Skruj's growl wasn't audible beneath another of Chivi's hearty laughs.

"I'm sure it's a pleasure to teach such a beautiful young lady. I wouldn't be in a hurry to get through those lessons either. Now come along, there are some people I want you to meet. You remember Corday, don't you, Eben?"

"Isn't he the one who kicked the ball through the headmaster's window?"

For the first time a smile crossed Skruj's face and... wow. She'd thought he was attractive before, but a smile transformed him. The smile softened his angular features, his sensuous lips formed an appealing curve, and those golden eyes lit up.

"The very same," Chivi said. "I'm sure he'd love to meet you again. You know he was also the one who..."

Continuing to recount the other male's escapades, Chivi guided them through the foyer and into the grand ballroom beyond. Columns ringed the outer walls, supporting a glass ceiling that soared high overhead. Some trick of technology allowed a full view of the stars overhead despite the lights of the ballroom below. Tables were arranged around the edges of the room, and at the far end, a set of wide steps led to a raised platform where a band played, the music a pleasant backdrop to the chatter of the crowd.

The entire room was tastefully decorated for the season. Evergreen garlands intertwined with tiny lights climbed the columns, and colorful arrangements of flowers and ornaments topped the tables. She couldn't help a twinge of envy at the festive decor—this was what she wanted for Timmy. But even if she couldn't give him anything so grand, perhaps she could pick up a few ideas.

"This is beautiful," she murmured, smiling up at Skruj, and he actually returned the smile, watching her face. Chivi nodded appreciatively as he glanced around.

"Indeed it is. Most importantly, the refreshment table is close at hand. Can I get you a drink?"

"Chivi!" A tall, broad-shouldered male broke away from a nearby group and approached them, his hand outstretched. "So good to see you."

"Corday." Chivi pumped his hand enthusiastically. "Look who has finally come to join us. Do you remember Eben?"

Corday's eyes widened.

"Of course. It's wonderful to see you again, Eben."

"Eben," someone else purred in a seductive voice, and Bobbi turned to see an elegant Londrian female had joined them. She disliked her on sight.

"How nice to see you again, Eben. Welcome back to Zenith."

"Thank you, Fellida."

He had stiffened again, but he spoke politely enough and she squeezed his arm in encouragement. His muscles flexed under her hand and then his hand covered hers. She saw Fellida's eyes track the gesture, her expression unreadable.

"This is Bobbi, Eben's companion," Chivi said. "Isn't that a nice surprise, Fellida?"

Fellida's expression suggested the only surprise was that Bobbi had been allowed to enter the Academy, but she nodded graciously.

"Of course. Welcome to Zenith Academy," Fellida said, her voice cool.

"Thank you."

"Are you enjoying yourself so far?"

"Very much."

Despite the rather chilly reception from the other female.

"Excellent. And how long have you and Eben been a couple?"

"Umm—"

She hadn't been prepared for such a direct question and she fumbled for an answer before Skruj came to the rescue.

"Several months."

His voice was equally cool, and she blinked up at him. Had she done something wrong? But his harsh gaze was on the other female.

"Congratulations."

There was just the slightest hint of skepticism in Fellida's voice, but Bobbi gave her a wide smile.

"Thank you. We're very happy together."

"You are? I mean, of course you are," Fellida said quickly. "I'm sorry. I was simply... surprised."

"We are private individuals." Skruj's voice had turned icy again. "We don't feel the need to broadcast our activities."

The female paled slightly, and there was a brief awkward silence before Chivi stepped into the gap, his voice a little too hearty.

"Now, who's ready for a drink?"

"No, thank you." Fellida had regained her composure. "Well, it is a delight to see you, Eben. Perhaps you might give me the chance to speak to you later."

"I am sure I will have an opportunity to speak to everyone," he said noncommittally.

Fellida clearly didn't like the answer, but she nodded and moved gracefully away.

"She never changes," Corday muttered, then grinned at Chivi. "How about those drinks?"

CHAPTER 6

*S*kruj watched Bobbi laughing at something Chivi had said, her expressive little face radiating happiness. Part of him wanted to hoard those smiles for himself, but he had somewhat begrudgingly admitted that there was no harm in the other male. In fact, he had clearly taken the two of them under his wing, shepherding them around the room and introducing them to old acquaintances. Perhaps because of those introductions, the reunion had not been quite the ordeal he expected.

A rather surprising number of people remembered him and, even more surprisingly, did not seem disturbed by his presence. If anything they seemed glad to see him, and in exchanging reminiscences, he had realized that not all of his time at the Academy had been unpleasant. He had simply forgotten the happier years. Even though he had entered as a poor orphan— both rarities—his classmates had not been unkind. At least not at first.

His claws flexed as he remembered that last terrible year.

"May we speak now?"

How appropriate that Fellida should appear just as his memories soured—she had been directly responsible for much of his unhappiness.

"I have nothing to say to you."

"Really?" Long elegant fingers gripped his arm, so different from Bobbi's gentle touch. "I have always... regretted how things ended between us."

He took a quick step back, leaving her hand to dangle uselessly between them.

"You ended them," he reminded her.

"You misunderstood the situation." Her gaze skittered away. "But perhaps you can find it in your heart to forgive me?"

"Haven't you heard? I have no heart."

Her lips firmed and her eyes flashed with temper before she attempted to soften her gaze..

"I have heard about you. Of how successful you've become."

She moved closer, the cloying scent of her perfume washing over him as she reached for him again, and he shook his head in disgust.

"I'm not interested."

Her lip curled. "Because of some human?"

"Yes. A human who is far more appealing than you will ever be."

She'd never taken rejection well, and he could almost see her gathering the insults to fling at him, but then Bobbi was there, taking his arm and giving Fellida a sweet smile.

"Sorry to interrupt but Eben promised to take me back to get some more of those delicious little cakes. Didn't you, snookums?"

For some reason the ridiculous nickname helped calm his repressed rage, and he relaxed a little.

"Of course."

"You should be careful, my dear. I hear humans are prone to gaining weight." Fellida delivered the barbed remark with a smile.

"Oh, I'm not old enough to have to worry about that yet. But I quite understand why you can't join us."

Bobbi's barb hit the target much more successfully. He saw Fellida's eyes flash again before he quickly tucked Bobbi against his side.

"Please excuse us."

"What a terrible female," Bobbi muttered as he quickly guided her away. "Most of your friends are charming, but not her."

Friends? He didn't have friends; he had acquaintances. But he'd had friends here once, although Fellida was not amongst them.

"She was never my friend." Bobbi gave him a curious look and despite his better judgment, he found himself continuing. "We were once engaged."

Until she decided that an inherited title was more interesting than a nameless orphan, no matter how good his prospects.

Bobbi's mouth dropped open, and his gaze focused on that appealing little circle, his mind conjuring up an unexpectedly erotic image of feeding his cock between those pretty pink lips. Shocked by both the thought and his body's immediate response to the idea, he would have turned away if her hand hadn't still been on his arm.

"To that bi... female?" She slowly shook her head. "And here I was thinking you were an intelligent male, snookums."

"Would you stop calling me that?"

She grinned up at him, and damn if his cock didn't stiffen even more.

"I think it suits you." She laughed again at his soft growl. "Now, you promised me cakes."

He led her to the dessert table, watching with amusement as she debated her choices before popping a small shougar in her mouth, an ecstatic expression on her face as she bit into it. She seemed to enjoy everything so much. What would it be like to be that... open to new experiences? Coming here had reminded him that he had been that way once.

Before I knew better, he reminded himself as he recognized an all too familiar laugh behind him. Fellida's betrayal had only been the start. Even though he'd thought he'd put it aside long ago, the memory of that pain threatened to resurface before he shoved it ruthlessly away.

Enough of this foolishness. His required hour had long since passed. Time to go.

"We're leaving."

"Oh." She gave him a startled look, but didn't argue. "All right. Do you want to say goodbye to Chivi and Corday?"

"No." He had no intention of seeing them again so why waste time on pleasantries.

Her small chin rose.

"Well, I intend to say goodnight. They've been very nice—to both of us."

He opened his mouth to order her to obey him, then reconsidered.

"I will get your cloak. Meet me at the front doors as soon as you have said your goodbyes. Make them quick. I'm not paying you for lengthy farewells."

"Fine."

She glared at him and marched away, her head high and her curvy little ass swaying provocatively beneath the tight gown. For a moment he was tempted to go after her, but he pushed the impulse aside and stalked off to the cloakroom.

He was waiting impatiently for the attendant when he heard that hated laugh again, this time followed by a bored, arrogant voice. *Lord Tarbell.*

"Did you see that poor Ebenweener had the nerve to show up tonight?"

His fists clenched, his claws digging into his palms.

"You can hardly call him poor these days. I hear he's one of the richest males in the city."

The second mocking voice was almost as hated. Lord Bellen. The two had always hunted together. He couldn't see either of them from the alcove where the cloakroom was located, but he knew their sneering faces all too well.

"His wealth makes no difference. He'll always be a poor motherless bastard to me."

How many times had that insult been flung at him that last year?

"I heard he brought a human to the reunion." Bellen chuckled. "Can you imagine?"

"I saw her. She's a fuckable little thing," Tarbell admitted begrudgingly.

Skruj's claws clenched hard enough to draw blood.

"Better than that bitch Fellida, anyway. Glad you finally got rid of her, Tarbell."

"I should have done it years ago. But now that I'm a free male, let's leave this dump and go find some more interesting females. Maybe even a human or two."

Bellen laughed, and the voices faded away.

"Master Skruj, I apologize for keeping you waiting. I have your cloak."

The attendant's return snapped him out of his shocked fury, and he realized he was about to drip blood on the polished marble floor.

"I'll be back," he snapped and strode quickly to the side entrance and out into the gardens, his only desire to get away.

He found himself on the path that circled the reception building and ended up outside the ballroom as he wiped away the blood. *A fitting metaphor*, he thought bitterly, standing alone in the cold and watching other people's happy lives.

Except he wasn't alone. A small warm hand curled around his.

"Here you are. When you didn't show up at the doors, I decided to come looking."

Her voice didn't sound reproachful, only soft and concerned, and he shuddered, his hand automatically gripping hers. They stood there in silence for a few minutes as his tension slowly eased. As it did, he finally noticed that her fingers were trembling.

"Is something wrong?"

"J-just a l-little c-c-cold. F-f-fine."

Damn. He'd been so caught up in his own misery that he hadn't realized she wasn't wearing his cloak. He quickly pulled her against the warmth of his body. She didn't object, pressing closer as her arms slid around his waist.

"That's better," she said with a sigh as he ran his hands up and down her arms, her skin cool and silky beneath his fingers.

Her breath brushed against his chest as she spoke, and his cock responded. He knew he should push her away before she realized, but she was still cold. She sighed, her voice muffled against his chest.

"What happened? I saw you head outside just as I was coming to meet you."

"Bad memories."

To his relief, she didn't ask any more questions. She just tightened her arms around his waist, almost as if she were... hugging him? And he... didn't hate it. He put his arms around her, holding her delicate body against him. Delicate, but also soft and feminine, and once again his body responded. He loosened his grip, intending to release her, and then she looked up at him, her eyes sparkling in the moonlight, and smiled.

He kissed her.

He didn't plan it. He didn't intend it. But he couldn't prevent the urge. She tasted of the shougar cakes she'd been eating and of sweet, innocent delight, and before he knew it, his tongue was seeking out every inch of her mouth. Her hands were clutching at him, her slender body trembling as her head fell back, and he wanted her. Wanted to possess her. Wanted to bury his aching cock deep inside her.

He wanted... her.

And that realization was enough to snap him out of his lust.

He lifted his head, his breathing unsteady as he stared down at her.

"Time to go."

His voice came out harsher than he'd intended. She blinked a few times, her eyes slightly unfocused, and then nodded.

"All right."

She spoke quietly, and for some reason he couldn't explain, his chest ached.

"Come."

This time his voice was gentler, and he carefully tucked her hand in his arm and headed back towards the reception hall. They collected his cloak and he wrapped it around her before they made their way silently back along the outdoor pathway, her silence no doubt due to the cold. Or at least that's what he told himself.

Littima was waiting at the end of the path with the vehicle, his expression carefully neutral as he drove them back across the city. They spent the entire trip in silence, each lost in their own thoughts.

His mind was filled with confusion. Now that this event was over, he should be focused on more important matters. Instead, he found himself focusing on the kiss—a kiss that had been... surprisingly pleasurable. More than pleasurable, if he were honest. And the way she'd responded, her slender body melting against him, her mouth deliciously sweet and responsive. As if she enjoyed kissing him...

Or did she think that was part of her contract, even though he'd been quite clear that it was not? Fuck. She was proving to be a distraction he didn't need. Damn Jakoba and his ridiculous schemes.

He had a company to run. He needed to concentrate on the upcoming expansion. If everything went according to plan, the entire planet would be using his services within a generation. He was already rich—soon he would be powerful as well. He would prove he was no longer the powerless boy who had attended the Academy.

"Do you want to talk about tonight?" she asked eventually, her voice still soft.

He was so preoccupied with the kiss that it took him a moment to realize that she was probably referring to the other events of the evening.

"No."

She looked over at him, her head tilted thoughtfully to one side, but didn't say anything. He had the sudden reckless impulse to tell her everything—how Fellida had pursued him, only to betray him with Tarbell, and how Tarbell and his friends had made his life hell after that. But it was in the past now. He'd graduated with honors in spite of their harassment and taken the training position in the bank, and now he had more money than God.

"No," he repeated unnecessarily, and a smile crossed her face for the first time since they'd entered the vehicle.

"I get the message. No talking necessary."

Her gaze dropped to his mouth, and her small, delicious tongue swept across her lips. Had she been thinking about the kiss as much as he had?

I'm only thinking about it because it has been such a long time, he assured himself as he turned away from the tempting sight to stare out the window. Not because it had any real impact on him.

They drove through her neighborhood, still bright and noisy at this time of night, and pulled up in front of her boarding house.

"The next event is one week from tonight." His voice sounded unusually loud in the silent vehicle and she started.

"I remember. Is there anything you want me to know about it? Or will it be a surprise as well?"

Was she reproaching him? Then he saw the gleam in her eyes and realized she was teasing him. How long had it been since anyone had dared such a thing?

"It is the annual celebration for the Londrian Finance and Economics Association. There will be a formal dinner."

"A formal dinner? I don't have any experience with that type of thing."

The teasing look had vanished, replaced by worry.

"I have every faith in your ability."

She looked up at him, her gaze startled and... pleased?

"I'm glad you think so. What about clothing? You said I can't wear the same dress to any of the events."

Unfortunately, she was right. And if what she had told him about the cost of female clothing was correct, he would have to advance a much larger sum than he'd anticipated. He started to reach for his wallet, then hesitated. He believed she was trustworthy, but he had learned long ago that he was not always correct about people.

"I will make arrangements and contact you later this week." He hesitated. "Also, the payment for tonight has been transferred to your account."

"Oh." A startled look crossed her face before she grinned at him. "I had such a good time that I completely forgot. Thank you."

She forgot? She had enjoyed the evening?

He could think of nothing to say, but she didn't seem bothered by his silence. Instead, she shocked him even more by leaning forward and brushing a quick kiss against his lips.

"Thank you," she whispered again, and then she was gone.

His hands flexed, fighting the urge to drag her back against him, and instead he watched as Littima, who had been waiting patiently for the conversation to be over, escorted her up the steps to her house. Before she entered, she said something that actually caused a hint of a smile to cross his steward's normally stoic face.

I should have escorted her. Next time he would. Next time...

For the first time in many years he found himself looking forward to something other than the next business deal, and when Littima returned to the car, he too was smiling.

CHAPTER 7

*B*obbi closed the door behind her and leaned back against it with a sigh just as Mrs. M'gid peeked out into the hall.

"There you are, dear. How was your evening?"

"Confusing."

Perceptive dark eyes studied her face.

"Is that why you're back later than I expected? Is everything all right?"

"I'm fine," she said quickly. "Mostly confusing in a good way."

That kiss had certainly been good. Better than good. Admittedly it had been a long time since she'd been kissed, but she couldn't remember one so... intense. His mouth had been so desperate, so demanding, as if he wanted to devour her, but his hands had been gentle. And she'd wanted more—until he pulled away so abruptly.

She blushed when her attention returned to the present, and she found Mrs. M'gid giving her a skeptical look.

"Really, I'm fine," she insisted. "Just a little tired."

"Go on up to bed then. You can tell me all about it tomorrow."

She gave the other female a grateful smile and slowly climbed the stairs. Kaba, the oldest M'gid daughter, was sitting on the couch reading, and she looked up and smiled as Bobbi entered.

"Did you have fun?"

"I did," she said truthfully. The setting had been beautiful, the food delicious, and other than the obnoxious Fellida, everyone had been very nice to her. And even if she wasn't entirely sure what to think about her encounter with Eben, she didn't regret it.

"How was Timmy?"

"Fine, although I couldn't get him to eat very much." A shadow crossed the girl's face before she gave Bobbi a hopeful look. "But he seemed in good spirits and he's been sleeping soundly."

"That's good." She crossed over to the desk and retrieved a small coin from the box she kept there. "This is for you."

Kaba shook her head vigorously.

"I can't take that. Mama said we were just being good neighbors."

"I know you are, and I couldn't ask for better, but I want you to have this. Treat yourself to a little something special."

The girl hesitated, then gave her a shy smile as she took the coin.

"Maybe I'll just save it so I can buy a dress like that one day. It's so pretty."

"It is, isn't it? And look!"

She twirled, sending the full lower part of the skirt flaring out around her, and they both laughed. Then Kaba left, and she went to check on Timmy. As the girl had promised, he was sleeping peacefully, and she gently kissed his forehead before going to her room.

Despite a sudden wave of exhaustion, she found herself thinking about Eben as she removed her dress and brushed out her hair. The contrast between the young boy who had enjoyed playing ball with his classmates and the cold businessman who had hired her was hard to reconcile.

And yet, despite that coldness, she had caught glimpses of a softer side, and the kiss had been anything but cold. Perhaps the problem was that he simply needed practice, she thought, remembering the way his mouth had felt against hers.

No. That was a very dangerous train of thought and one she did not intend to pursue. He had hired her for three events and then she would never see him again. And it wasn't as if she had time for a male in her life, especially not one as complicated as Eben.

Despite her conclusions, her dreams were filled with images of Eben—and they did much more than kiss. She woke early, still aroused from the erotic imagery that had filled her dreams. Her breasts ached, and she cupped them gently in her hands, brushing her thumbs across the taut nipples and relishing the resulting spike of pleasure. How long had it been since she'd thought of herself as anything other than a worker and a caregiver?

Timmy's birth had been hard on her mother, and her health had never really recovered. Bobbi had been looking after Timmy almost from the moment he was born—not that she'd ever regretted it, but it hadn't left much room for a social life. At the time when other girls were going on their first dates, she'd been changing diapers. And then the news about Earth's destruction and the subsequent announcement that they would be sent to another planet had destroyed any hope of a normal life. Even on the ship she'd been too busy caring for her mother and Timmy to spend much time with anyone her own age.

So maybe it was understandable that she'd have a little trouble resisting an attractive, powerful male who had actually kissed her.

But now it was time to stop daydreaming and get to work. She had a late shift today, and she intended to get a head start on her Christmas plans now that she had some extra credits. Giving her breasts a quick, regretful squeeze, she climbed out of bed. If she wasn't too tired tonight, maybe she could take a little time and remember how it felt to pleasure herself.

TWO NIGHTS LATER SHE WAS REGARDING THEIR decorating achievements with a smile. Mr. M'gid had helped them bring home the small tree now standing proudly in front of the window. She'd added colored lights and a set of pretty ornaments while Timmy had made a long paper chain to wrap around it. There was no fireplace and Londria didn't have a tradition of hanging stockings, but she'd found a pair of colorful oversized men's socks and hung them from the dresser knobs. She'd already picked up a few small items for Timmy's stocking and concealed them in her room.

Her communicator suddenly buzzed, and she gave it a startled look. The device was an expense she could ill afford, but she'd had to make sure that she could be contacted if Timmy needed her. She'd opted for the most basic plan and hoarded the minutes carefully, rarely using it. With Timmy safely in his room, who would be calling her?

"Hello?" she asked cautiously.

"Roberta." So they were back to that. The deep voice still sent a pleasant shiver down her spine. "I have been considering the matter of your next outfit. I have decided it would be most efficient if I were to accompany you to the clothing store."

He was taking her shopping? She tried to picture him standing in the frothy pink decor of the store where she'd bought her last dress and failed miserably. But if that was what he wanted...

"Umm, okay. When?"

"Tomorrow. I will arrive at thirteen hundred hours."

"I can't do it tomorrow. My landlady is taking her family out of town for the day to see relatives. I don't have anyone to watch Timmy. Is there another time we can do it?"

"I have meetings scheduled for the rest of the week." There was a long silence. "Your brother could accompany us."

"Are you sure? He tires easily."

"I wasn't intending to embark on an extended expedition. I simply wish to purchase a dress and a cloak. How long could it take?"

It had taken her over three hours to find the first dress, but that was partly because she had been trying to find something for the limited amount of credits he'd provided. *Maybe it will go faster this time,* she thought doubtfully. And although she doubted Timmy would enjoy watching her shop, he would enjoy seeing more of the city decorated for the holidays.

"Will Littima have your vehicle nearby if Timmy gets tired?"

"Of course."

"All right. We'll be waiting."

"I'm look... Yes."

He abruptly ended the call, leaving her staring at the comm. Had he been about to say he was looking forward to seeing her? A slow smile curved her mouth before she went to tell Timmy about the outing.

He was surprisingly enthusiastic, and peppered her with questions about Skruj. She hadn't realized until that moment that she knew very little about him other than that he was wealthy and... complicated. Timmy grinned and held up his datapad.

"Let's look him up."

There was surprisingly little information available, other than lists of the companies he owned and business deals that he'd made. As far as she could tell, he was never mentioned in any of the social columns. So why had he decided to attend the events for which he'd hired her?

"It says here he developed the design for a new type of encryption system, and that his bank was one of the first to use the system," Timmy said excitedly. "He must have lots of money. He owns all kinds of companies and stuff, including the biggest bank in the city."

"I suppose he does, but I don't think it's made him happy."

"I'd be happy with that much money. I could buy a scooter and a new game and more books."

Her heart ached at the longing on his face. She wished she could give him everything he deserved.

"Would that make you happy, monkey? If it also meant you were all alone?"

Those green eyes, so like her own, flashed to her face and then he shook his head.

"No, I wouldn't like that."

"Neither would I." She hugged his thin shoulders. "And we do okay, don't we?"

"Yeah, sis. I don't need those things."

But now she would have enough credits to give them to him. She hugged him again and turned back to the data pad.

"Let's see what it says about the Londrian Finance and Economics Association."

Hmm, it appeared to be primarily devoted to education and networking. She had a sneaking suspicion that this would be another event that he had not previously attended. Was he just making a statement or was there something else behind his decision?

"Look, Bobbi, he's got an award!"

Sure enough, Eben's name was on a list of awards given to students who had distinguished themselves. He had been the top of his class and had received an award for innovation. If he'd done so well, why had he been so reluctant to return to the Academy?

"He's pretty smart," Timmy said with a sigh.

"So are you."

"Maybe, but I never got a prize."

And with his irregular attendance, he probably wouldn't even though he was smart enough to keep up with his class anyway.

"You deserve one, monkey. I'll tell you what, why don't we see if there are any new games out?"

His eyes lit up before he bit his lip.

"Really? But we don't have the credits."

Her chest ached again. He deserved so much more than she could give him.

"I have enough this week."

She'd already put aside a few credits to pick up a small treat for him. He gave her a quick, fierce hug.

"Thanks, sis."

She returned the hug, silently vowing to make this his best Christmas ever.

CHAPTER 8

S kruj stared up at the boarding house where Bobbi lived, torn between regret and anticipation. The very fact that he was anticipating seeing her again made him wary. *This is a business relationship, no more,* he reminded himself yet again. The shopping trip had simply seemed like a reasonable compromise between his desire to see her suitably dressed and his reluctance to hand over a large number of credits.

"Would you like me to let Miss Bobbi know that we are here, Master Skruj?" Littima asked quietly.

"No."

He had regretted not escorting her to the door on their last visit —he did not want to make the same mistake this time. As he climbed out of the vehicle, a small Zyran child on a hoverboard almost collided with him.

"Sorry, master."

The child grinned and dashed off again, while a Zyran female gave him an apologetic look. She was sitting on the steps of the house next door talking to a neighbor. Farther up the street a group of males were arguing about the last drone race while three young girls were drawing pictures on the sidewalk. A late flowering vine spilled over the fence of another garden in untamed abundance, and the scent of fried food drifted by. It was so very different from his street, but the people around him looked far more content than the brief glimpses he'd had of his own neighbors.

He climbed the steps thoughtfully, only to find himself looking down at a small Coomar child. Of course, she shared the house with others.

"Can you direct me to Roberta's rooms?"

Big dark eyes regarded him suspiciously.

"I mean Bobbi's rooms."

"Up there." She pointed up a set of interior stairs and dashed off.

He sighed and climbed up to the next floor. Two doors opened out onto the landing, neither of them marked, so he knocked on both. One of them opened immediately to reveal a big Tiwan scholar frowning at him.

"I am looking for—"

"For me," Bobbi said breathlessly as she opened the other door. "Sorry, Master Xant."

The scholar's face softened slightly, before he bowed politely and retreated back into his rooms, and Bobbi winced.

"Oops. He always seems to be working, so I try not to disturb him."

"Your door was not marked and the child did not tell me which one was yours."

She grinned.

"That must have been Kami. She's not very talkative. But I need to talk to you privately anyway."

Slipping out into the hallway, she pulled the door closed behind her. He suddenly realized that she was only wearing an oversized robe clearly intended for a male. Her small feet were bare and her hair was piled on top of her head in a loose knot, damp tendrils curling around her bare neck. She flushed as his eyes trailed over her and pulled the robe tighter across her chest —which only served to emphasize her small, high breasts and the stiff little peaks thrusting against the thin cloth.

Once again his body responded with one of those unwelcome surges of excitement, but he refused to acknowledge it.

"Sorry. I just got out of the shower. It's been a hectic morning— which is why I wanted to talk to you. Kadra, the M'gid's oldest boy, had an accident this morning. It wasn't anything serious, but it meant their trip out of town was postponed until this afternoon."

"And this is important because?"

"It means Timmy could go with them after all. It's just..." Small white teeth clamped down on that luscious lower lip. "I had already told him he was coming with us and he's very excited about it. Do you mind if he comes anyway?"

Yes. He would much rather be alone with her. Then again, he would much rather carry her back into her rooms, strip away that ridiculous robe, and explore every inch of her warm, damp body... *Fuck.* Perhaps having a third party along would prevent him from doing something foolish like kissing her again.

"He may come."

"Oh, thank you."

She gave him a radiant smile, rose up on her toes to kiss his cheek, and dashed back into the apartment while he was still trying to decide how to respond. So much for not kissing her...

She kissed me, he assured himself, but the brief press of her lips had only made him hunger for more.

"Come on in," she called. "I'll be ready in a minute."

He took a deep breath—and then regretted it when her sweet fragrance filled his head, adding to his unwelcome arousal. He did his best to force his cock to behave and entered her home.

The small living area was bright and cheerful, the furniture worn but clean, and the room had been carefully decorated for the holiday. His gaze swept over the colorful decorations, and then came to an abrupt stop. Sitting at a desk at the other end of the room was a small boy, regarding him gravely. His coloring was entirely different from his sister's, but those eyes were unmistakable.

"Master Skruj."

He nodded.

"You must be Timmy."

"Tim, please."

They stared at each other, and he realized why Bobbi worried about the boy. His skin looked far too pale, even for a human, and he was painfully thin, but those eyes burned with a fierce intelligence.

"You don't need to take me," Tim blurted out. "I'm fine here."

"I suspect your sister will not agree," he said dryly. "She tells me that you wish to see the sights."

He saw the flash of longing before a stubborn little chin went up in a familiar gesture.

"I don't need to see them."

"But perhaps your sister does."

"Maybe," Tim agreed. "But you don't."

"Perhaps not. But it will please me to show them to her." The words held an uncomfortable ring of truth. "To both of you," he added quickly.

The boy studied him, then nodded as graciously as a ruler condescending to a servant, and Skruj had to bite back a smile.

"Thank you," he said solemnly.

"I'm ready." Bobbi came flying back into the room. "I told you it wouldn't take long."

She had donned a soft red upper garment that clung lovingly to her small breasts and brought warmth to her skin. Pants in some worn blue material were equally snug, showcasing her long, slender legs. The clothing was not Londrian, but it was undeniably flattering. Unfortunately, she was carrying that wretched pink coat over her arm.

"Leave that coat."

Her chin came up, mirroring her brother's early gesture.

"It's cold outside."

"You are only going from the house to the vehicle and then the vehicle to the store."

The chin didn't budge, and he sighed.

"I will purchase a proper winter coat for you. Consider it a bonus," he added when she frowned. "The weather is only going to get colder for the next few months, and you won't be much use to... anyone if you're sick."

"Oh, all right," she muttered ungraciously. "But nothing expensive."

He had an even harder time concealing his smile this time.

"Of course not. Shall we go?"

Tim was fascinated by his vehicle, asking a number of surprisingly intelligent questions, and he was equally surprised to find that he didn't mind answering them. He directed Littima to drive through the park so they could admire the decorations, as well as all the preparations for Last Night. Tim's eyes widened at the enormous pile of wood that was being assembled.

"Do they really light all that?"

"Yes. The fire must burn from dusk on Last Night until sunrise on First Day to welcome in the new year."

"Wow."

Afterwards they drove slowly down one of the main shopping streets beneath the colorful garlands strung from building to building and admired the elaborate window displays. When

Littima brought the vehicle to a halt in front of the store he'd selected Bobbi's eyes widened.

"I don't think you want to go here," she whispered. "It's ridiculously expensive."

"I know." He'd researched it extensively. "It's also the most highly regarded. I wish to... make an impression."

After an extensive argument with himself, he'd decided that if he were going to attend these events it would be foolish to conceal his wealth—and he wanted to see Bobbi in one of the elaborate creations he had seen in his research.

"If you're sure," she said doubtfully.

"Of course."

The three of them walked into the store, and an older Zyran female immediately approached them. She was impeccably dressed, her face smooth and expressionless as she bowed.

"May I help you?"

"We require a formal gown—red, I think—with a matching cloak, plus an everyday coat."

Her gaze flicked over to Bobbi.

"Is there time for alterations?"

"Only one day."

"I can raise the hem if necessary," Bobbi said quickly, and the saleswoman's face softened slightly.

"No need, my dear. A day should be sufficient. Come with me. There is a seating area for the gentlemen," she added firmly.

She suddenly reminded him of the housekeeper from his academy days. Mrs. Trottwell had a kind heart, but she brooked no nonsense from any of the boys.

"Yes, madame," he said meekly as he and Tim obeyed.

She led Bobbi away and they settled themselves in a small alcove with a view of the fitting area. A small tray with beverages and treats appeared in front of him, and Tim eyed it hungrily.

"Eat whatever you want."

"Really?" Tim glanced at him, his eyes hopeful, then reached for a small pastry. "Thank you."

Skruj hid his smile and poured a drink for each of them.

Tim watched the proceedings curiously, commenting on each gown and cloak and sometimes offering suggestions. The saleswoman was a stern taskmaster and Bobbi tried on many more garments than Skruj thought were strictly necessary, but she looked delectable in each one. He was trying to decide which he preferred when she appeared in a final option.

"That one," he said immediately.

Intricate beadwork covered the bodice and rose into stiff points above her shoulders. The beads shimmered as they caught the light, creating the illusion of flames licking up the fabric. An underskirt of heavy red silk clung to her slender hips, but delicate layers of tulle, intricately embroidered with flame motifs and highlighted with more beads, floated over it.

"It's pretty," Tim agreed, then yawned.

"Are you tired, monkey?" Bobbi immediately asked.

"Tired of dresses," the boy muttered under his breath, but shook his head. "I'm fine, sis."

"If you're sure." She didn't look as if she believed him, but she didn't argue. Instead, she turned to the saleswoman. "Can you give us a minute, Marletta?"

"Of course, miss."

As soon as the female vanished, Bobbi hurried over to him..

"This isn't the right dress," she said urgently, her breasts swelling delightfully against the low neckline.

"Why not? It suits you perfectly." Not only did the color flatter her, but the slender lines of the dress accentuated her graceful figure.

"I heard one of the other saleswomen talking. It's the most expensive dress in the whole shop. And with all the hand stitching, the alterations alone are going to cost more than a week's salary."

"You are trying to save me credits?"

"Well, of course."

He couldn't help it—he started to laugh. She stared up at him with such an adorably puzzled look that he was almost tempted to kiss her again.

"I consider it an investment," he told her, soothing his own conscience.

"Really?"

"Yes. People always prefer to trust their credits to someone who is already successful, and if my... companion is well dressed, my success is clear. That is, do you like the dress? I want you to enjoy wearing it."

"Like it?" Her hand traced down the bodice in an unconsciously seductive gesture. "It's the most beautiful dress I've ever seen."

"Good, then the matter is settled." He glanced over at Tim, swinging his legs restlessly. "Perhaps you can decide on a coat more quickly?"

"I think I already have," she said, her voice apologetic. "It's one of the less expensive ones. But it's pretty and it's the one that I liked the best."

"That is acceptable."

"All right." She flashed him a relieved smile. "I'll try it on and then we'll be done."

She disappeared behind the screen, and when she emerged, he understood her choice. The coat was made of soft wool and dyed a deep, rich green, while the collar and the cuffs were trimmed with white fur.

"Definitely that one," he approved, and her smile returned, brighter than ever.

"Thank you."

He ignored the way that smile sent a rush of heat through his body and led her back over to where Tim was waiting.

"Are we ready to leave now?"

"Could we do one thing before we go?" She gave him a mischievous smile and gestured towards the side of the shop. "I saw a rack of hats and scarves over there. I thought I could get Tim a scarf now and you could deduct it from my next payment?"

"That is not necessary. Go ahead."

She hesitated, then gave him a quick nod.

"Thank you. Tim, would you like to come and pick something out?"

The boy jumped off the seat and followed his sister, leaving him free to pay the bill.

"My... companion needs more clothing," he said quietly to the saleswoman. "Please arrange a line of credit for her—she may purchase whatever she wishes."

He no longer had any doubts that she would abuse the privilege. In fact, he suspected it would be difficult to get her to take advantage of the opportunity. The female shot him an unreadable look, then nodded.

"Of course, sir."

Bobbi and Tim were waiting by the door for him, Tim proudly displaying his new scarf. Bobbi had a small bag clutched in her arms and she held it out to him.

"What is that?"

"A scarf for you."

When he didn't take the bag, she pulled out the scarf and held it up. An intricate pattern of bright colors was woven into the thick wool, and he gave her a stunned look.

"Me? You got that for me?"

"Yes, of course. Marletta told me these are traditional colors for Last Night. It's supposed to bring you luck in the new year."

He swallowed, hard.

"I didn't know that."

"Now you do. Here, let me put it on you."

Speechless, he bent down and allowed her to wrap the soft material around his neck, her scent filling his senses. She carefully tucked the ends inside his collar, then smiled up at him.

"Perfect."

He couldn't resist. He put his arm around her waist and kissed her. Conscious of Tim's interested gaze and the public surroundings, he kept it brief—just a quick taste of her sweetness, and perhaps... a promise of more.

CHAPTER 9

"In here," Bobbi said quietly, leading the way into Timmy's room.

Eben followed her, carrying the sleeping boy, then placed him gently on the bed. She slipped off his shoes but didn't bother with anything else before pulling the blankets over him. She returned to the living room to find Eben pacing, a frown on his dark face.

"I should not have taken the two of you ice skating."

"Yes, you should have," she said firmly, going to him and putting a hand on his arm. "It made him so happy."

"But it wore him out."

"I know." She sighed and turned away, tempted to start pacing herself. "He's easily exhausted, but I still want him to have fun and he did."

So had she. Watching as Eben carefully showed Timmy how to skate, first supporting him from the side, then skating backwards in front of him as easily as if he were walking on a road. Timmy had been flushed and triumphant when they returned.

"Did you see that? I skated all by myself!"

"You certainly did. I'm very impressed."

She handed him a cup of the Londrian hot drink that was almost like hot chocolate and wrapped a thick fur rug around his thin shoulders. Not only had Eben brought them to the outdoor rink after a wistful comment from Timmy, he had procured one of the private heated huts overlooking it.

"You were pretty impressive as well," she told him. "It obviously wasn't your first time."

"No, I learned a long time ago." From the smile lingering on his face, it was a pleasant memory. "Do you skate?"

She laughed.

"I've been on skates before, but I wouldn't go as far as saying I know how to skate."

"I would be happy to guide you."

"Yeah, go on, sis. It's fun."

"Will you be all right waiting here?"

"Of course I will."

He rolled his eyes at her, so much like a normal little boy that her chest ached, but she forced a smile to her face as she turned to Eben.

"All right. But you'd better not let me fall."

"I won't," he promised, and he hadn't.

He had whirled her around the rink to the music playing from the tinny speakers as night settled over the city and the stars came out. Old-fashioned torches illuminated the edges of the rink, burning with a sweet scent, and it had been... magical. And even more magical when the music slowed and he pulled her closer, waltzing her across the ice with his strong arm firm around her waist and his golden eyes glowing down at her. For a brief moment it was just the two of them and the stars and the music.

But then the dance had ended and he'd cleared his throat and stepped back. But he kept his arm around her waist as they skated back to the hut to find Timmy half asleep in a nest of furs. He was fully asleep by the time Eben's vehicle brought them back and Eben had refused to let her wake him, insisting on carrying him upstairs.

"What is wrong with him?" he asked abruptly, jerking her back to the present, and she sighed.

"I wish we knew." She paced over to the small kitchen. "Would you like a glass of wine? Mrs. M'gid made it."

Despite the obvious doubt on his face he nodded, and she poured two small glasses of the deep ruby liquid and carried them to the sofa, gesturing for him to sit down. He took a cautious sip, then nodded.

"This is excellent."

It was, rich and fruity with a lingering warmth, and she took another sip.

"He was a fussy baby but some babies are, especially when they're born early. I didn't worry about it that much until we got to his one-year checkup and he was still much smaller than he should have been. The doctors back on Earth suspected there was a problem with his immune system, but they couldn't pinpoint the cause."

"What about on the transport ship? Surely they had more advanced technology."

"Yes, but less experience with humans." She made a face, remembering some of those frustrating conversations. "It didn't help that there weren't many medics and they were always busy. He also doesn't seem sick much of the time. He gets tired easily, catches every disease that comes along, and he's still way too small for his age, but they seem to think he'll grow out of it. But he isn't growing out of it! And I'm so afraid that he's just going to... slip away."

Her voice broke on the last words and she took another hasty sip, determined not to give in to tears. She looked over to find him staring at his hands, his face unreadable.

Perhaps, like most males, he was simply uncomfortable with illness. Her father certainly had been—or at least that was the excuse he gave.

"What of the doctors here?" Eben asked slowly, and she sighed.

"The free clinics are like the medical units on the ship—busy and understaffed—but I did manage to convince one of the doctors to get him an appointment at the teaching hospital in the spring."

"The spring?"

He looked as outraged as she had been and she managed a smile.

"That was my reaction as well, but apparently I was lucky. Most of the appointments for non-critical cases are a year out."

"And you're sure today didn't harm him?"

"I'm positive. He wants to do all the things that other boys do and today, you gave him that. Thank you."

He was only a short distance away on the small sofa, close enough that she could feel the warmth of his body and catch that faint spicy scent that always surrounded him. She slowly put down the glass of wine, then leaned over and kissed him.

At first his lips were unresponsive beneath hers, but she refused to give up, sliding her hands around his neck and deepening the kiss. His mouth parted, allowing her to slip her tongue inside, and he tasted just as delicious as she remembered. Warm and spicy, with a hint of the sweet wine. His hand came up, cupping the back of her head, and then he took control of the kiss, plundering her mouth, his tongue mating with hers.

Arousal pulsed between her legs, her breasts aching and heavy as she squirmed against him and he groaned. He pulled her onto his lap, settling her needy pussy directly over his massive erection, and her body responded instinctively, her hips rolling as she rubbed against his cock. A wave of pure, intense pleasure washed through her and he groaned as she cried out against his lips.

"Oh, gods, Bobbi."

His big hands slid down her back and over her bottom, pulling her even closer as his mouth found hers again. He devoured her, his mouth hot and hungry, and she responded just as eagerly. His hand slid up under her sweater, big and warm and possessive as it closed around her breast, so much better than her own hand, and she moaned, leaning into that firm grip as he rolled her nipple between his fingers.

"Perfect," he whispered against her mouth, and bent her back over his arm.

His mouth trailed down her throat, nipping and licking, before he yanked her sweater up and sucked her nipple into his mouth. She cried out, her hands clutching at his hair as the exquisite sensation shot straight to her pussy.

"More, please."

He obliged, his tongue lashing her sensitive bud until she thought she might explode, and then he moved to the other nipple, repeating his ministrations while she panted and squirmed in his lap. His cock was still hard against her core, but it wasn't enough. She pressed impatiently against the thick ridge of his cock, and he growled approvingly.

"Yes. Oh, yes. More. Please."

She was babbling, grinding her wet, swollen pussy against him, and she didn't care. He shifted her position, his hand sliding between their bodies and cupping her, and she moaned again. There was a distant ripping sound, and then a shockingly large finger slid through her slick folds. Her hips bucked helplessly as he explored.

"Tell me what you need," he demanded, just as he brushed against her clit.

"There. Right there."

She thought he smiled against her breast, but she was too focused on that big finger steadily circling the swollen nub to be sure. He dipped lower and suddenly pushed his finger deep inside her, filling her completely, and she cried out at the stretching pain.

His cock jerked beneath her, but he kept his pace slow and steady, pumping his finger into her slick channel as his thumb found her clit again. Those golden eyes stared down at her, full of lust and approval, and the combination sent her over the edge. Pleasure flooded her, washing over her in waves as her pussy spasmed around his finger.

He stroked her through the aftershocks and then finally withdrew, leaving her empty and aching.

"Was that... good?"

He sounded so uncertain that the warm haze that had surrounded her dissipated and her eyes flew open. His face had resumed its usual stern mask. She knew him well enough by now to recognize that he used that mask to conceal his own emotions, but it still made her embarrassingly aware that she was sprawled across his lap with her sweater up around her neck and her jeans... Her jeans had been ripped apart at the crotch.

"What happened to my jeans?" she asked as she quickly yanked her sweater down and scrambled off his lap.

He held up his hand and flexed it and those dark, dangerous claws appeared. She gulped.

"Oh. I guess that explains it."

"I apologize for the damage," he said stiffly. "I will arrange to have them replaced."

He started to rise, and she suddenly realized she'd never answered his question.

"Wait."

She tugged on his hand and he reluctantly settled back down, his muscles rigid with tension.

"I'm sorry, Eben. I just didn't expect things to happen that quickly."

"I apol—"

She reached over and put a finger over his mouth.

"Don't. It was quick, but it wasn't unwanted." She stroked her finger across that sensuous lower lip. "It was very much wanted. And to answer your question, it was also very, very good."

His mouth curved beneath her finger, and then he shocked her again by sucking gently at the tip. Her breasts tingled with remembered pleasure and she started to lean towards him again, but he stopped her.

"I think perhaps I should leave. This is becoming... complicated."

An unwilling snort of laughter escaped her.

"That's an understatement. But it's not a bad complicated, is it?"

"I... I don't know."

If anyone else had said that after a similar encounter she would have been hurt and furious, but although her chest ached, it was on his behalf.

"All right," she said quietly. "Perhaps you should go."

"Yes," he agreed, but he didn't move.

She waited, watching as the war on his face settled into something resembling resignation.

"You will still attend the dinner with me?"

"Of course. We have a deal, snookums."

He finally smiled and shook his head.

"I still do not like that name."

"But it still makes you smile." She rose, wincing when her torn jeans fell to the ground, and held out her hand. "Come on. I'll walk you to the door."

He took it, the warmth of that contact searing her, and rose also. Hand in hand they walked to the door, and then he hesitated again.

"May I kiss you goodnight?"

"Oh, yes," she sighed as he put his arms around her.

The kiss started off tentative, but then she nibbled on that tempting lower lip. He growled, and the next thing she knew her back was up against the wall and his cock was grinding against her as he devoured her mouth. Her legs came up to circle his waist, and he froze. Very carefully he put her down on her feet and stepped back.

"You are a very dangerous female, Roberta."

Despite the arousal humming through her veins, she grinned at him.

"Thank you."

He shook his head, but he was smiling as he finally left. She stumbled over to the couch on suddenly shaking legs and collapsed.

"What on Earth am I going to do now?"

CHAPTER 10

*S*kruj sat in the back of his vehicle, his claws tapping impatiently on the upholstery. It had been two days since the... incident and he hadn't seen Bobbi since then. He had called her twice, merely to check on Tim's health he'd told himself, and each time they had spoken for almost an hour. She'd told him more about her past—much of which infuriated him—and he'd wished he could have been there to watch the emotions dancing across her expressive little face as she talked. And now he would be able to see her—if they ever arrived.

"Doesn't this vehicle go any faster?" he snapped.

"Yes, Master Skruj. The other traffic, however, does not."

Littima's voice was as calm and untroubled as always, but Skruj heard the note of amusement and sighed.

"Sorry."

"It's just holiday traffic, sir. We will arrive in good time."

And indeed they did, but it felt as if hours had passed before the vehicle drew to a halt. He didn't bother waiting for Littima to open the door, impatient to see Bobbi. He strode up the steps and knocked sharply.

She opened it immediately, already wrapped in the red velvet cloak that matched her dress, and smiled up at him.

"You're early."

"And you're ready."

Her beautiful eyes sparkled up at him.

"Maybe I was anxious to see you again, snookums."

He put his arm around her velvet covered waist and drew her close.

"What will it take to make you forget that ridiculous name?"

Before she could respond, the door farther down the hall flew open and a family of Coomar tumbled out. He recognized the little girl who had answered the door, but the rest were new to him, especially the very large Coomar male who was regarding him suspiciously.

"Eben, this is the M'gid family—my landlords and very dear friends."

"We're very pleased to meet you, Master Skruj." The matriarch greeted him warmly, but her mate only grunted. "The two of you have a good time tonight and don't worry about a thing. We'll take good care of Timmy."

"Where is he?" he asked, looking around for the boy.

"Here I am." The boy dashed out of the hall door. "I wanted to give you this—to thank you for taking us skating."

He handed Skruj a haphazardly wrapped package and he felt a sudden lump in his throat.

"Thank you."

He carefully opened it and discovered a small painted ornament depicting a skating scene. It was made of cheap glass, but it was clear that someone had put a great deal of effort into the painting.

"Timmy made it," Bobbi whispered.

"It's perfect. Is that us?" he asked, tracing the small figures skating around the rink.

Tim beamed proudly.

"Yep. This way each time you decorate your tree, you can remember the time you taught me to skate."

"Thank you, Tim. I will treasure it."

The boy grinned and ducked his head, then dashed back inside the M'gid's apartment. The rest of the family followed, Mr. M'gid still glaring at him.

"Thank you," Bobbi said quietly.

"For what?"

"For not telling him that you don't have a tree."

"How did you know?"

"Just call it an educated guess."

She smiled up at him, her face so warm and understanding that he started to bend down and kiss her, reconsidering at the last moment.

"If I kiss you, I'm not sure we will make it to the dinner."

"It would be a shame to waste this dress," she agreed solemnly, and slipped her hand in his. "Dinner it is."

By the time they had joined the line of vehicles pulling up in front of the Civic Center, he was having second thoughts.

If it hadn't been for the conditions of the will, he would have ordered Littima to take them home.

"What's wrong?" Bobbi asked. "More bad memories?"

"No, these are all current. I know many of these people, but I do not like them and they do not like me."

"Why not?"

"Because they are constantly asking me for things I do not care to give. Time for their meetings, credits for their charities, even locations for their meaningless activities."

"What kind of activities?"

"Does it matter?" he demanded impatiently.

She didn't respond, green eyes fixed on his face, and he finally sighed.

"This year they want to use one of my empty warehouses to host a holiday camp for disadvantaged children. To feed them sweet treats and help them make useless ornaments..."

Fuck. The realization swept over him.

"They meant ornaments like the one Tim made for me, didn't they?"

"I expect so. If it hadn't been for this job, I wouldn't have been able to give Timmy those things either. Is that useless?" she asked, pointing to the small box holding his hand-painted ornament.

"No," he growled. He didn't like this feeling of guilt that was sweeping over him. His old mentor would have laughed at such foolishness, and yet... "I'll let them use it."

Small fingers curled around his, but she didn't say anything. Some of his anxiety about the event disappeared, and he was almost smiling when they finally reached the drop off point.

This time they only had to walk a short distance under a lavishly decorated canopy to reach the front doors. Uniformed servants bowed them in, then offered to take their cloaks, but he waved away the one who addressed Bobbi.

"I'll do it."

He didn't want anyone else's hands on her. She smiled up at him as he unfastened the clasp at the neck and his breath caught. She had looked beautiful when she tried the dress on, but now it had been tailored to fit her slender body perfectly. The beaded flames on her bodice flickered as her breathing sped up, her eyes still fastened on him.

"Beautiful," he whispered, and her cheeks flushed pink.

"You look pretty beautiful yourself." She ran her hand over the vest he'd chosen, dark red satin embroidered with flames to match her gown. "I like this."

His body started to respond to the gentle caress, and he covered her hand with his own.

"Be careful. Do you want me to throw you over my shoulder and carry you out of here?"

Her eyes widened, and then she gave him a slow, seductive smile.

"Maybe."

He glanced at his wrist comm. An interminable fifty eight minutes to go.

"Dinner first," he muttered, and she laughed.

"Whatever you say, snookums."

Damn if his cock wasn't starting to respond every time she used that ridiculous name.

"Dinner," he repeated desperately and tucked her hand in his arm.

The dinner had not yet started, and the guests were milling around a large wood paneled room. Chandeliers sparkled overhead, illuminating the elaborate decorations, and more uniformed servants circulated carrying trays of drinks and appetizers.

He recognized far too many of the people there, and with a resigned sigh he approached Dartron, the leader of the group who had approached him about the warehouse.

"Master Skruj." The male's voice was cold, but scrupulously polite. "I did not expect to see you here."

"Eben told me about all the wonderful things you're doing," Bobbi said cheerfully. "So I insisted we come."

Dartron's eyes widened, and then he bowed gracefully.

"I'm sure no one could refuse a request from such a beautiful young lady."

Smooth bastard. He drew Bobbi firmly back against his side.

"I have reconsidered. You may use the warehouse."

"Really? Why, that's wonderful. We've been having a devil of a time finding an appropriate location." Dartron beamed happily. "Are you responsible for that as well, young lady?"

"Oh, no. It was all Eben's idea."

He shrugged uncomfortably. "Just don't leave a mess."

"Not at all. We'll make sure everything is neat and tidy."

They wouldn't, of course. But it was worth it to see the happiness on Bobbi's face—and to know that someone like Tim would have a place to go.

"I think they're getting ready to announce dinner," Dartron said and Skruj turned to see the hostess taking her place at the entrance to the dining room.

"We'd better find our table," he murmured, and Bobbi nodded, smiled at Dartron, and followed him to the doorway.

The big dining room glittered under another impressive set of chandeliers, fine crystal and highly polished cutlery reflecting the lights. Low clusters of flowers on each table were interspersed with tiny bubbles of light that added to the festive scene.

They took their seats just at the table they'd been assigned near the front of the room—due to his wealth, no doubt. It certainly wasn't because of his popularity.

"It looks like you two are seated at our table," a tall Londrian female said as she approached the table. Her eyes swept over

Bobbi and dismissed her. "And you must be Master Skruj. I am Dina Garnet."

"Delighted," he said dryly, and reluctantly held the chair next to his.

Her eyes brightened and she took the seat, settling her skirts gracefully and giving him a dazzling smile.

"How very thoughtful. You'll have to tell me all about yourself," she said, patting his hand.

"There is nothing to tell," he said coldly, and she finally withdrew her hand, her expression hardening.

No wonder he hated these events.

"And so we meet again."

Chivi's infectious laugh drew a genuine smile from him as the other male approached.

"I see the beauteous mistress Bobbi is even more dazzling this evening," Chivi continued, bowing low over Bobbi's hand.

"And I see you are as smooth talking as ever. Are you joining us?"

"Happily so." Chivi glanced over at the female next to Skruj and his smile faded. "Dina."

"Good evening, Chivi. What a pleasant surprise."

Her tone implied it was anything but, and Bobbi quickly spoke up.

"Yes, it is. You didn't mention you were coming when we were at the reunion."

"Last minute change of plans. I made a small donation to one of their outreach programs and they insisted."

Skruj seriously doubted it had been a small donation—Chivi had been foolishly generous even back at the Academy. And yet he looked far more content with his life than Skruj had been. The other male was chatting genially with Bobbi when he suddenly stiffened.

"Oh, dear. I'm afraid dinner may be a little tense."

CHAPTER 11

*S*kruj turned around to see what had caught Chivi's attention and froze. Lord Tarbell was approaching, a pretty and very young Londrian female on his arm. The boy he'd once been wanted to flee, but he forced himself to remain seated. *I have wealth and I have power. He has no hold over me.*

"Nonsense. Ancient history." He forced his voice to remain neutral.

"Of course," Chivi murmured, clearly skeptical.

Bobbi was obviously confused, but she reached under the table and took his hand. Her touch soothed him and he even managed to keep his face calm when Tarbell reached them.

"Well, well, well. What an... interesting gathering. The Association must be quite desperate for guests."

"Indeed. All it seems to take is a meaningless title," he said coolly.

To his satisfaction, Tarbell's supercilious smile faded, but Dina jumped hurriedly into the breach. Apparently she had some sense after all.

"I'm delighted to finally meet you, Lord Tarbell. I'm Dina Garnet. Your sister and I went to school together."

"Indeed? You look far too young to be a compatriot of my sister's."

"You're too kind," Dina simpered. "We weren't close friends, of course, but I have admired her for many years."

"I'm sure." Tarbell's tone was just a shade short of rude. "Let me introduce you to Farn Harlow."

The girl at his side had been listening with a bewildered look on her face, but now she blushed and smiled at all of them.

"I'm very pleased to meet you."

Tarbell looked over his shoulder, but by now all of the tables were full.

"It appears we have no choice. Let me seat you, my love."

He bent solicitously over the girl who gave him a besotted look. Foolish female.

"She doesn't look very old," Bobbi whispered to him.

"She probably isn't. His... tendencies are well known."

An outraged expression crossed her face.

"What about her parents?"

"If I remember correctly, her father is a newly wealthy merchant. They have wealth but no status."

They wouldn't be the first to use a pretty daughter and a sizable bankroll to buy their way into the aristocracy.

"But why—"

"Later," he promised and turned back to the table.

"Aren't you going to introduce us to your companion, Eben?" Tarbell asked, and he could almost hear the hated nickname underlying his words.

"Roberta Cratchar, this is Lord Tarbell."

Tarbell studied her far too closely for his liking before smiling.

"What an unexpected pleasure."

"It's nice to meet you," Bobbi said, her voice flat, and immediately turned to Chivi.

It was the most uncomfortable dinner he'd ever had. Tarbell kept making thinly veiled insults, smiling the whole time, while Dina did everything but grab Tarbell's cock to get his attention. His pretty companion simply looked confused. Bobbi was unusually silent, clearly picking up on his tension, and several times she took his hand under the table. Only Chivi was his usual self, providing a gentle stream of conversation in a vain attempt to relieve the tension.

When the dessert was finally cleared, the hostess took her place at the podium and began the long process of thanking the donors and awarding prizes. The room buzzed with conversation, and he finally felt his shoulders relax. As soon as the speeches were over, they could leave.

Bobbi excused herself to accompany Farn to the restrooms, and Chivi took her place next to him.

"Well, this has been interesting," Chivi murmured under cover of a round of applause and he shot him an irritated look.

"That's not how I would describe it."

"Of course not. But the evening has not been a complete waste."

It had been as far as he was concerned, and he frowned at his friend.

"How can you say that?"

"Because you did not let Tarbell's behavior drive you away."

He supposed that was a triumph of a kind.

"You do realize that he's actually jealous of you, don't you?"

"What? That's ridiculous."

"You were smarter than him at the Academy and Fellida chose you first. That's what turned him against you back then. Now you're richer than him, and you have a much more entertaining companion," Chivi added with a smile as the ladies returned and he let Bobbi resume her seat.

"She's seventeen," she whispered furiously. "Seventeen! And they're engaged."

He sighed. "I don't like it either, but she seems happy about it."

The girl was giving Tarbell more worshipful looks.

"I know. I tried to suggest she should wait until she was a little older, but she didn't want to hear it."

"I agree it's a shame, but I don't think there's anything we can do about it."

Bobbi glared across the table, but Tarbell only looked amused as Farn whispered in his ear.

Skruj found himself thinking about Bobbi's fierce expression rather than the speech. She might look delicate and sweet, but her protective instincts were formidable. No doubt they'd had to be to bring up her brother mostly on her own.

Thankfully, the speech ended shortly afterwards and everyone rose to leave.

"Thank the gods that's over," he muttered and Bobbi gave him a sympathetic smile.

"Are you ready to go?"

"Absolutely."

Other than Chivi, the other occupants of the table had already left and his friend accompanied them as they made their way slowly through the crowded lobby. Skruj looked around and sighed.

"I'll go get our cloaks. It will be faster than waiting for the servants. Will you stay with Bobbi, Chivi?"

"We'll be right here. Unless I can convince her to run away with me."

He knew the other male was teasing, but his claws still flexed. Chivi grinned and raised his hands.

"I'm just a harmless old bachelor, remember?"

"See that you stay that way," he snapped.

Chivi's laughter followed him and he found himself grinning as he headed for the cloak room. The front counter was mobbed, but if he remembered correctly, there was a rear entrance. He found it and managed to snag an attendant's attention with a handful of credits. Cloaks in hand, he was about to return when he heard a familiar voice from the dark passage next to it.

"I said, on your knees."

"But, Tarbell, I don't understand." Farn's voice was shaking.

"You'd better learn to understand. Do you think that human hesitates when that bastard orders her to her knees? She probably even enjoys it. Down."

There was a soft pained whimper, but he'd heard enough. He dropped the cloaks and turned the corner. Tarbell had his fist in Farn's hair. She was crying and the neck of her gown was torn.

"Leave her alone, Tarbell."

"Why should I, Ebenweener? She belongs to me, don't you, my dear?"

Farn shook her head frantically, still crying, and Tarbell scowled, yanking on her hair.

"Oh yes you do. Your father made a deal with me."

"Let her go," he repeated.

"Or what? Do you think you can defeat me in battle?"

"I'm not intending to try. I'm simply going to tell your future in-laws exactly what you just told your betrothed."

Tarbell froze, his grip on the girl's hair loosening.

"You wouldn't dare. I've already signed a contract with them."

"I most certainly would tell them, and I doubt they're desperate enough for a title to go ahead with the marriage. Let her go."

Tarbell finally released Farn, and the girl stumbled into his arms, her face stained with tears.

"Go," he urged and she ran.

"I'm not going to forget this, Ebenweener," Tarbell snarled and he shook his head.

"Isn't it time you found a new nickname?"

Tarbell's fists clenched, and he tensed, ready for the attack, but instead, Tarbell stalked away.

He bent down and picked up the cloaks, thinking about his old nickname. Ebenweener. Eben the loser. Well, he was no longer a loser. He was rich and successful and... respected. Perhaps, just perhaps, it was time to forget his past as well.

Bobbi was standing right where he'd left her, Chivi hovering at her side. Her eyes widened as she caught sight of him.

"What happened to you?"

"Oh, dear," Chivi said, and then laughed.

"What's so funny?"

"Nothing," Chivi said quickly. "Not at all."

"I had an encounter with Tarbell," he growled, and Bobbi's mouth formed a small O.

"What happened?"

"Later. Here, let me put your cloak on."

"But..."

He waited while she searched his face.

"Never mind."

She held out her arms and he fastened the clasp at her throat, resisting the urge to bend down and kiss the side of her neck.

"Thank you, Eben," she said softly.

"You're welcome, Bobbi."

Chivi was still grinning, but he didn't care. He tucked her arm in his and escorted her outside, her sweet scent filling his senses.

"Would you like a lift, Chivi?" he asked.

"No, thank you. I have other plans. Enjoy your evening."

Chivi disappeared back into the crowd as they climbed into the waiting vehicle.

"You seem happy," she said softly.

Happy? He considered the idea.

"Perhaps 'at peace' is more accurate."

She smiled and took his hand, examining his fingers.

"Did you really fight with Tarbell?"

"It didn't come to blows, but I confronted him."

"Why?" she asked, studying his face.

"Because I didn't like what he was doing to that girl."

"That was nice."

"I didn't do it because it was nice. I did it because he disgusts me."

"But you did do it. That's what counts. And it doesn't matter why you did it, just that you did."

Perhaps she was right.

"I suppose."

"So you won, then? You got her away from him?"

"Yes. Although I can't promise she won't go back to him if he turns up with gifts and apologies."

She sighed.

"I suppose not. But maybe she won't be as naive this time."

He put his arm around her shoulders and pulled her closer.

"I don't want to talk about them anymore."

Her eyes widened and she licked her lips.

"What do you want to talk about?"

"I don't want to talk at all." He traced her pretty lips with his finger. "I want you to come home with me."

Her tongue flicked out again to lick at his finger, and then she smiled.

"All right."

"Just like that?"

"Just like that."

He reached for the control panel.

"Littima, if you can get us home in less than fifteen minutes, I'll double your Last Night bonus. Less than ten and I'll triple it."

CHAPTER 12

*B*obbi's heart pounded as they entered the big, silent house. They hadn't spoken for the rest of the very fast drive, and she could see the tension in Eben's body. *But I want this.* And she did, desperately, but it was hard to hide her nerves as he guided her up the stairs and into a large bedroom with dark wood paneled walls.

It was as bare as his office, the only furniture a single chair and side table in front of the fireplace and an enormous four-poster bed with heavy, dark blue velvet drapes. Matching curtains covered the windows and the only light came from two small sconces on either side of the bed. Her pulse thundered in her ears as she stared at the bed.

"Are you sure about this, Bobbi?" he asked, his voice strained, and she jumped.

Somehow she managed to pull herself together enough to smile at him.

"Why do you think I asked Mrs. M'gid to let Timmy spend the night?"

She tried to speak lightly, but even she could hear her voice trembling. His eyes flashed gold.

"If we're going to stop, we need to stop now," he growled.

"No stopping. Not unless you're the one who wants to."

"There's absolutely no chance of that, sweet."

"Good." She started to take off her cloak, then hesitated. "Do you want to do it?"

He growled again and stepped forward, reaching for the clasp. But instead of removing her cloak, he pushed the velvet aside and slid his hands over her breasts. His big fingers gently explored the curves before his thumbs found her nipples and stroked them. Pleasure spiked through her, her pussy pulsing in response, and she gasped.

"Your breasts are perfect. Just the right size to fit in my palms."

He squeezed the small mounds and she arched her back, offering them up.

"Please," she whispered.

His fingers closed around her nipples, pulling and twisting, and her legs wobbled. She reached for him, and he finally removed the cloak. He let it drop to the ground as he swept her up in his arms and carried her to the bed, lowering her down so gently that she wanted to cry. He stepped back and removed his cloak and his jacket, and then stood, frowning.

"What's wrong?" she asked, and he smiled.

"I'm not sure how to get you out of that dress. There are so many fastenings."

"I can do it," she said, returning his smile. "Mrs. M'gid helped me put it on, but I can take it off myself."

"Not this time. This time I'm going to undress you."

His voice was firm and her breath caught.

"All right. There are clasps up each side, and then there's a ribbon keeping the overskirt in place. It will be easier if I stand."

He nodded and pulled her to her feet before untying the over-skirt and letting it fall to the ground in a cloud of fabric, the embroidered flames glittering even in the dim light. She reached up and took the pins out of her hair as he started on the tiny fastenings up each side of the dress, his touch sending little sparks through her with every brush of his fingers. When he was finished, she turned and lifted her loose hair, letting him loosen the final clasp. The dress slipped to the ground and he turned her back, his golden eyes glowing.

"You are so beautiful," he murmured, and her cheeks warmed.

"I don't think I'm anything special," she said.

"I do. And you are not allowed to contradict me. Not now. Not here."

She shivered at the command in his voice, but gave him a teasing look.

"Yes, snookums."

"Don't call me that."

He shook his head, but he grinned as he stroked her cheek.

"What shall I call you then? Master Skruj?"

He scowled.

"Just Eben. I like it when you say my name."

"Eben," she breathed, and his eyes flashed again.

"Turn around."

He was still fully dressed, his voice and expression stern. The heat between her thighs intensified, and she slowly obeyed.

"Good."

He stepped behind her and raised her arms up and back.

"Now hold on to me."

He was so tall, she had to stretch to reach his neck, but it was worth it when he began exploring her exposed body. He started down over her shoulders, his fingers skimming across her skin until he cupped her breasts.

"Such pretty pink nipples."

"They're just breasts," she mumbled, the pleasure of his hands distracting her.

"*Your* breasts. Your perfect breasts."

He pinched her nipples, rolling the hard buds between his fingers, and her head fell back against his chest as a moan escaped her.

"That's right. Just relax."

She didn't know how to do that, but she could focus on him. On the solid, warm body behind her and his clever hands. He tugged at her nipples and her pussy ached, wet and needy. One big hand slid down her stomach, and her knees almost buckled when he cupped her.

"I love the way your soft, pink folds part for me," he whispered in her ear, his voice low and hungry. "Show me more."

She opened her legs wider, giving him access, and he immediately plunged a finger deep inside. Her slick inner muscles tightened around him, the pleasure almost painful.

"Gods, you're so tight."

"Is that bad?"

"Definitely not."

He gave a choked laugh as he withdrew his finger, making her whimper. Then he slid his finger into his mouth.

"Fuck, you're sweet."

He gently disengaged her hands from around his neck and turned her towards the bed.

"Hold on to the post."

She was expecting his hand to return between her legs, and when his hot, wet tongue licked at her entrance, she almost collapsed. Only the reminder of his order kept her upright.

"So sweet. Do you like this, Bobbi?"

"Yes," she managed.

"And when I do this?"

His tongue swirled around her clit and she moaned.

"God, yes."

He hummed with satisfaction, the vibration making her quiver, and then his big hands wrapped around her hips, holding her steady as he feasted. His tongue and lips teased and tormented, but always dancing around her clit, never quite pushing her over the edge. She tried to wiggle, to force him to give her what she needed, but he was too strong.

"Eben, please."

His tongue brushed over her aching clit, and she almost cried.

"Yes, yes. More."

He gave her exactly what she wanted, and more. She moaned as his tongue fluttered over her throbbing flesh, driving her closer and closer to the edge. Then his finger thrust deep inside her and the combination was too much. Pleasure crashed over her, and she sobbed his name, her legs buckling. He caught her easily and laid her gently on the bed.

She opened her eyes to find him gazing down at her, his face softer than she'd ever seen it.

"Beautiful."

He kissed her gently, and she tasted herself on his lips. Satisfaction filled her as she smiled up at him.

"You're wearing far too many clothes."

"I agree."

His vest joined her dress on the floor, followed by his shirt. Then his pants hit the floor and her mouth fell open.

"Oh my."

He was huge, long and thick and perfect. The same golden lines that covered his skin also covered his cock, but here they pulsed softly. He looked far too big for her, but the ache between her legs intensified and she reached out her hand to him.

He joined her on the bed, leaning over her, and she felt the head of his cock brush her stomach. She shivered in a rush of excitement and nerves. He kissed her, his hands running possessively over her body. When his thumb found her nipple again, she gasped and arched her back.

"Do that again."

"Greedy little thing," he chuckled, but did as she asked, tugging and teasing until her pussy was throbbing and the room was filled with the scent of her arousal.

"You smell so sweet." He inhaled deeply as she blushed.

He kissed her again, his mouth hungry and demanding, his tongue thrusting in the same way his cock was thrusting against her stomach. His cock was leaving a damp trail, and the knowledge that she was making him feel this way sent another wave of desire through her.

"Eben," she whimpered, and he grinned at her.

"One more."

He rolled to the side and lifted her on top of him. Her body was pliant and yielding, her mind still hazy from her last orgasm, and she frowned in confusion.

"But—"

"Trust me."

"I do. But—"

"Lean forward. Hold on to the headboard."

Her breasts were now right above his face, and she watched in dazed fascination as he opened his mouth and sucked a nipple inside. He bit down gently, the sharp prickle of his teeth sending a new jolt of pleasure through her, and her hips bucked. His cock rubbed against her stomach, leaving another damp trail, and then he guided her down his body until his cock nestled between her folds.

She slowly slid up and then back down. She was so wet, so ready, that it wasn't difficult to glide back and forth along the thick shaft. Each time she slid upwards, his mouth was there, his teeth and tongue working her nipples until her entire body was tingling.

"Enough," he growled finally, and wrapped his hands around her waist.

She found herself flipped onto her back, his big body looming over her. She waited, her heart pounding, but he didn't enter her.

"Tell me this is what you want."

His voice was harsh, commanding, and she shivered with anticipation.

"More than anything."

He growled and slid his cock into her opening, stretching her as he breached the tight ring, and the slight burn made her gasp. He stopped immediately.

"Am I hurting you?"

"N-no."

"Tell me the truth."

"You're not hurting me," she said more firmly.

He pushed a little further, his cock stretching her even more, but he stopped before the burn became too much. She could feel his markings pulsing against her inner walls, teasing her most sensitive areas, and then he withdrew. He pushed back in a second time, then again and again until she moaned, lifting her legs and wrapping around his hips.

"More."

He thrust forward, burying his cock deep inside her in one hard stroke, and her mouth fell open again, too shocked by the sudden, overwhelming fullness to cry out. He didn't move as her body struggled to adjust. Her pussy fluttered wildly around the massive invader, and his markings pulsed, massaging her clit from inside her body. The burn faded, but the fullness remained. She gave a slight experimental wiggle, and he slowly began to move.

"Gods, you feel good."

His voice was harsh, but his hands were gentle as he touched her, his hips pumping slowly and steadily. Her body tightened, her need building again. Her legs tightened around his hips, urging him on, and he obeyed. His hips snapped forward and the first flutterings of her orgasm started.

"Oh, God. Don't stop."

He kept up the fast, demanding pace until pleasure overwhelmed her, her body shuddering as she called out his name. He kept thrusting, the aftershocks turning her shudders into waves of pleasure, and then he growled, his claws pricking her skin as he exploded deep inside her, the rush of heat triggering another tremor.

He didn't pull out, but he rolled to his side, taking her with him. She sighed, a blissful feeling of contentment filling her, and pressed a kiss to his chest. His arms tightened as he kissed the top of her head in return.

"Perfect."

"It really was," she murmured, and fell asleep in his arms.

CHAPTER 13

*S*kruj woke to a soft, warm female curled up next to him—an event that had never happened before. The few times he'd indulged in a physical encounter, it had been no more than a brief interaction, the only goal to relieve his physical needs. Last night had been so much more.

Too much more, a voice whispered. *She's a distraction.*

How many times had Towlin, his old mentor, advised against any involvement with a female?

"Females are nothing but trouble. Don't make the mistake of losing your heart to one."

Fresh from Fellida's betrayal, the words had fallen on fertile soil. He had devoted himself to business instead and had succeeded far beyond his wildest hopes. But each success, each company acquired or account increased, only left him wanting more. And now he realized that his old mentor had been right. Bobbi was a distraction. Not just because of her sweet, willing body, although he could happily wake up like this every morning, but because he didn't want her to go home.

I don't want her to leave.

The thought shocked him. He'd never wanted anyone to live with him before.

"Stop thinking so hard. It's too early," Bobbi muttered.

"My apologies. Go back to sleep."

"Not without you."

She snuggled closer, and he allowed himself to push aside his concerns—for now—and just enjoy her presence. He was smiling when he followed her into slumber.

When he awoke again, her side of the bed was empty and only the scent of sex lingered in the air.

She left me.

The desolation that filled him at the thought only confirmed his earlier suspicions. She was a distraction—one that made him vulnerable. The idea made him uncomfortable, and he rolled over to discover that his discomfort wasn't entirely mental. His cock was rock hard, his markings pulsing with need.

He groaned and reached for her pillow, breathing in her lingering scent.

"Bobbi?"

He called out hesitantly, but received no response. Had she left the house entirely? Surely Littima would have woken him if she'd wanted to leave. He wasn't going to go chasing after her like some lovestruck schoolboy.

Instead, he headed for the shower, hoping that the pounding water would cool his lust. But his markings only grew more demanding, the pulses making his cock jump and twitch despite his attempt to ignore it.

He gave up the fight and stroked his cock. A wave of relief swept over him, but only for a moment. His hand was no substitute for her hot, tight little body and the pulses grew stronger, more insistent, the rhythm matching his strokes.

He was panting, his hand flying up and down his shaft, but his markings were not satisfied. They kept growing hotter and hotter until he had to pull his hand away. His cock was swollen and pulsing so rapidly that it seemed to vibrate.

"Bobbi," he groaned.

"I'm here."

Her sweet voice answered from the bedroom, and he sighed with relief. She hadn't left him.

"Come here."

She stepped through the doorway wearing the shirt he'd been wearing the previous night. A surge of possessive heat filled him at the sight, but he also noticed that it left her legs bare and she was clearly naked beneath it and he frowned.

"Where did you go dressed like that?" he demanded.

"To the kitchen to get us some tea and toast. Don't worry, Littima wasn't there."

She smiled as she came towards him, but then her eyes widened.

"What's wrong?"

"My markings are reacting to your presence. I need you."

She swallowed nervously, but her pretty little nipples were already hard, pressing against the thin fabric of her shirt.

"Please," he growled, and she nodded.

Her hands went to the hem of the shirt but he shook his head.

"Leave it," he ordered, and she obeyed, joining him under the stream of water, the shirt immediately turning transparent.

"That looks painful," she said softly, and hesitantly reached for his cock.

He groaned, the touch of her hand a relief but also making his marking throb even harder.

"Am I hurting you?"

"Gods, no."

She smiled and stroked him again, harder this time, and his hips jerked forward. Then she shocked him by dropping to her knees.

"Bobbi..."

"Hush. Maybe this will help."

Her mouth closed over the head of his cock, her tongue immediately swirling around the head.

"Fuck," he grunted.

The soft, wet heat made his markings burn, and his claws flexed. He could come just like this, he knew it. And yet...

"Stop."

"But—"

He lifted her to her feet and carried her out of the shower and over to the vanity. Her reflection was wide-eyed, but her nipples were thrusting against the wet shirt. He tugged the bottom of the shirt up over her ass and gently pushed her forward until she was bent over the counter, her pretty pink pussy peeking out between her legs.

"Hands flat on the surface," he ordered, running his hands down her back and over her ass in a soothing caress.

She was panting now, her lips parted and her pupils dilated. His markings were screaming at him, but he could wait a moment longer.

"Wider."

She obeyed, the lips of her pussy parting to reveal that impossibly small entrance. He rubbed the head of his cock along the glistening flesh and they both groaned. Then he slid his cock inside her and all other thoughts were wiped from his mind.

"Perfect. So perfect."

She was wet and welcoming, her channel hugging him tightly, her inner muscles quivering around him. Her hands balled into fists on the vanity top as he withdrew and then slammed forward, seating his cock deep inside her.

"Eben!"

"So good."

His markings were blazing now, sending waves of excitement through him. His thrusts became faster, harder, each one burying his cock deeper. He slid his hand around to her front and stroked a finger over her swollen clit. Her tight little channel spasmed around him, her pussy clutching at his cock as she cried out his name. Pleasure washed over him, his cock jerking wildly as he pumped jet after jet of his seed deep inside her.

"Gods."

His knees threatened to give out, and he staggered back, pulling her into his arms as he collapsed to his knees. He was still buried inside her and he could feel her inner muscles squeezing him.

"Are you all right?" he asked, and she nodded, a faint smile curving her lips.

"Not exactly how I thought we'd start the morning. Not that I'm complaining," she added quickly.

He laughed, and then they both moaned as the vibration rippled through their still joined bodies. He leaned down and kissed her shoulder.

"Shall we go back to bed?"

Her smile widened.

"Whatever you say, snookums."

This time they made love slowly, but as much as he enjoyed the languid exploration, he became increasingly conscious of the fact that time was passing, that soon she would have to leave. That knowledge didn't stop his chest from aching when she finally sighed and sat up.

"I have to go. Timmy will be expecting me."

"Yes."

"One more event."

"Yes."

His tongue felt thick and slow, welded to the roof of his mouth. She hesitated, then climbed out of bed, looking down at the discarded dress.

"Do you mind if I raid your wardrobe again?"

"No."

He seemed to be incapable of anything other than one-syllable words, but she only nodded and disappeared into his dressing room. She returned a short time later wearing another one of his shirts over a pair of pants which she had rolled up. They were still far too big for her, but she'd wrapped a tie around her waist to keep them up.

"Not the most stylish outfit," she said dryly. "But with the cloak over it, no one needs to know."

I will know.

"Stay for breakfast," he said, suddenly finding his tongue.

She hesitated, then shook her head.

"I'd better not. It would only make it harder." Her smile wobbled. "Will I see you again before the next event?"

He should say no.

"I'm not sure."

"All right. Well, you know where to find me. Goodbye, Eben."

She gave him another shaky smile, and then she was gone. He wanted to howl out his pain and frustration. Instead, he did the same thing he'd done every morning of his adult life—he put on a suit and went to work.

CHAPTER 14

"*Y*ou're not listening," Timmy said accusingly, and Bobbi jumped.

"Sorry, monkey. What did you say?"

"I was telling you about the model I was building, but I'll show you later. You promised me pancakes this morning."

"Yes, I did, but come here first."

He rolled his eyes, but let her give him a hug. Did he feel even thinner than usual? She pushed aside the ever-present worry and smiled at him.

"Did you have fun last night?"

"Yep." He gave her a curious look. "Mrs. M'gid says you didn't get home until very late. She said to tell you that you need to eat something."

"Thank you. How about you help me make pancakes?"

"Cool. With berries?"

"Of course. Go get the bowl and we'll get started."

He was stirring the batter when he shot her a quick look.

"Is Skruj coming back around?"

He was obviously trying to sound casual, and her chest ached.

"I'm not sure. We have one more event to go to, but he's awfully busy."

"Oh." He stirred the batter slowly. "I thought I'd make him a Christmas present. Is that okay?"

"Of course it is."

"Good." He grinned at her and focused on the pancakes.

To her surprise, Eben called her that night. Unlike their previous conversations, it was brief and stilted but it gave her hope. Hope for what, though? She wasn't foolish enough to think there was a real future for them. He was a rich, important male, and she was a refugee who worked in a clothing factory. The time they'd spent together was magical, but that was all it was—an illusion of another life. It would end after the next event.

Even if he did decide he wanted to spend more time with her, she wasn't sure it was a good idea. Not only did she think her heart would be damaged, she was very afraid that Timmy would be affected as well. He already dropped Skruj's name into the conversation far too often. Not that she expected him to offer to spend more time with her, she told herself firmly.

And yet he continued to call each night until the night before their last date.

"Do you have a dress?" he asked.

"Oh, yes. And I think you'll find it acceptable." She hesitated. "Marletta told me what you did. It was very kind of you, but you know I can't accept."

There was a long silence, and then she heard him sigh.

"No, somehow I didn't think you would. I just... don't like to think of you going without."

"We're managing just fine."

He made a skeptical noise and went silent for so long that she was about to end the call.

"There's something else," he said finally.

Her heart skipped a beat.

"What?"

"I have already transferred full payment for the job into your account."

"What? When did you do that?"

"After we went skating," he admitted.

"But you didn't tell me."

"No. I wasn't sure if you would still accompany me. But for tomorrow night—I only want you to come if it's what you want."

She should say no, end this impossible relationship before any more damage was done to her fragile heart, but instead she found herself saying, "I want to go with you. Very much."

"Good. I'll pick you up at the same time."

She could hear the relief in his voice before he ended the call and left her staring at the communicator. He wanted her to choose him. Did that mean...

It means nothing, she told herself firmly. He's just being nice. But she went to bed smiling.

Once again she was waiting when he arrived, and once again Timmy was spending the night with the M'gid's. She tried not to think too hard about why she'd asked or the way Mrs. M'gid had studied her face when she made the request.

"Are you sure, dear?"

"Yes. But it's the last time. I don't want to take advantage of you."

"You're not. Timmy is a pleasure to have around."

"Thank you." She blinked back the tears and hugged the older female. "For everything."

Now Mrs. M'gid watched silently as she opened the door for Eben. She'd spent the week trying to convince herself that he wasn't as big and handsome as she remembered, but the reality was even better than she remembered.

"Bobbi," he murmured, golden eyes glowing.

"Hi."

She did her best to ignore the blush that was creeping across her cheeks.

"Hi, Skruj," Timmy said, rushing over to her side. "I made you a Christmas present."

"A Christmas present?"

"It's like your First Day celebration," she explained. "A time of hope and new life."

"I see. I am honored." He gravely took the small package. "Should I open it now?"

"Of course not. You have to wait for First Day."

"Very well. Thank you, Tim."

Timmy grinned and ran off again, leaving Eben looking after him with an odd expression on his face.

"He seems well."

"He had a bad spell earlier this week, but fortunately, it didn't last long."

"Why didn't you tell me?" he demanded and she shrugged awkwardly.

"It didn't come up."

He opened his mouth, then closed it again and offered her his arm.

"Shall we go?"

As soon as she put her hand on those warm, firm muscles, a thrill of remembered heat surged through her. She knew she was blushing again, but she did her best to ignore it as she waved goodbye to Mrs. M'gid and the children.

Littima was waiting by the limo and he smiled at her as he opened the door.

"Good evening, Miss Bobbi."

"Good evening, Littima."

Eben helped her in, then went around to the other side, but she was sure his hand had wanted to linger. Did she want it to? Did she want him to touch her?

Of course I do, she thought crossly. If this was their last night, she didn't want to waste it. As soon as he sat down next to her, she leaned over and whispered in his ear.

"Hello, snookums."

He groaned, and then she was on his lap as he kissed her with fierce, satisfying intensity, leaving her nipples aching and her pussy throbbing when he finally raised his head.

"Hello." He tugged gently at the neck of her cloak. "You look very beautiful tonight. Can I see your dress?"

"When we get to the event," she said firmly, even though she was tempted to say to hell with the whole thing and drag him back to his house. "What is this event, by the way?"

"Didn't I tell you? It's the groundbreaking ceremony for a future hospital. One of my companies has the building contract."

"You mean we're going to stand outside in the dirt while you cut a ribbon?"

He laughed and tugged her back against his chest.

"Not exactly. I think you'll like this."

He was right. They joined the now familiar line of vehicles curving into what at first appeared to be an open lot. Then they turned the corner and she gasped. A shimmering white pavilion appeared in the lot, but it wasn't a simple tent. Instead, ghostly towers rose from each corner with a sheer roof suspended between them. The whole structure looked like a replica of a much larger building.

"Is that what the hospital is going to look like?"

"Exactly. Do you approve?"

"It's beautiful," she said sincerely. And deceptive. As they stepped out of the vehicle and onto the white carpet leading to the entrance, she realized the walls of the pavilions towered far over her head. The actual hospital was going to be enormous.

The carpet was lined with displays of white flowers, and she grinned at him.

"I definitely chose the right dress."

"What do you mean?"

"You'll see."

As soon as they entered the flower-decked lobby, he pulled her to one side and reached for the fastening of her cloak. She laughed and let him remove it, watching his face as he looked at her.

At first glance the dress was deceptively simple—a strapless white gown with a full skirt—but as soon as she moved it came to life, the light revealing the intricate snowflakes embroidered on the bodice, each one unique. The snowflakes continued down onto the skirt, gradually becoming three dimensional and rising from the fabric as if she were walking in a cloud of glittering snow.

"You're right. I do like it. Very much." He trailed a finger along the low neckline, then tugged her back behind one of the ornamental trees. "Close your eyes."

"What are you up to, snookums?" she asked suspiciously, and he sighed.

"Just close your eyes, sweet."

She obeyed, and a moment later something cool and heavy settled around her throat. Her eyes flew open as she looked down at the necklace—diamonds woven into intricate snowflakes that drifted down across her chest.

"How did you know?"

"I didn't." He hesitated. "I was going to give it to you. Later."

Her throat threatened to close. *A parting gift.*

"You know I won't take it. But if you don't mind, I'll wear it tonight."

"I would like that very much."

She rose up on her toes and kissed him.

"Thank you."

"You're welcome." He traced the outline of the necklace to the lowest point just above her neckline and her nipples tightened. "It suits you. You should keep it."

"A factory worker has no use for a diamond necklace."

"But you don't have to work—"

"No," she said again, and changed the subject. "What do we do now? Dance? Eat?"

"Neither, thank goodness. All we have to do is walk around. There will be doctors scattered throughout to explain what their department will do."

Her heart skipped a beat. "Is there a children's department?"

"I'm afraid not."

She forced a smile. "Then let's see what they do have."

Most of the areas were surprisingly boring, but she enjoyed the obstetrics ward with pictures of smiling mothers and plump babies magically suspended in the semi-transparent walls. She'd always been too busy with Timmy to really think about it, but now a pang of longing hit her. What would it be like to have a child of her own? Maybe one with striking charcoal skin, patterned with gold.

Stop that, she told herself. It was just a foolish fantasy. But when she looked up at Eben, his eyes had heated. Was he imagining the same thing?

They moved on, passing through an experimental lab before entering the final department—a geriatric ward. Here too pictures filled the walls, this time of wise old faces, many of them smiling. Eben looked around casually, then suddenly froze.

CHAPTER 15

owlin. It can't be, Skruj thought desperately, but the face was unmistakable. Unlike most of the other portraits, he wasn't smiling but glaring out at the world with an all too familiar scowl.

Bobbi gave him a curious look, but didn't say anything as he studied the portrait.

"Ah, I see you're looking at one of my more interesting cases." A doctor walked over to join them. "Sad, of course, but very interesting."

"I thought he retired. To an island off the south coast." That had always been Towlin's plan.

The doctor frowned and shook his head.

"Not that I'm aware of. My records say that he continued to work until his heart failed. That's when I encountered him."

"You tried to help him?"

"There wasn't much I could do, I'm afraid. At that point we just try and make them comfortable." The male shook his head again. "Do you know not a single person came to see him? I think perhaps that's why he just gave up. Literally turned his face to the wall and gave up. I believe he willed himself to death."

"No one came to see him?"

"Not a soul. Usually we get someone, even if it's just an acquaintance from work. Did you know him?"

"Once. But we didn't keep in touch."

Towlin had always said impatiently that he had no time for sentiment.

"Hard to believe that a male can live so long and never really connect with another person. Perhaps that explains it."

"Perhaps."

"He did die a very wealthy male," the doctor added, then nodded and walked off.

Bobbi squeezed his numb fingers.

"Do you want to leave?"

"Yes."

He didn't know if they had been there a full hour, but at this point he just didn't care. He needed to leave.

Despite his urgency, it took some time for Littima to work his way back through the crowd of vehicles. He simply stood there waiting, and Bobbi stood next to him, holding his hand. As soon as they were back in his vehicle, he lifted her onto his lap and wrapped his arms around her, breathing in the sweet scent of her hair.

"How well did you know him?" she finally asked quietly.

"Not well at all. He didn't want to be known. But he was my mentor when I first left the Academy. He taught me everything I needed to know about running a business and being successful."

Towlin had never mentioned the dying alone part. He shuddered and tightened his grip on Bobbi. She didn't object, humming softly as she nestled against him. He didn't ask her to stay this time, just lifted her out of the limo and carried her up the stairs. He stripped away the beautiful dress with his claws and made love to her with fierce, silent desperation until she shuddered and cried out his name and his own release washed over him in long aching waves.

"He wouldn't have approved of this, you know," he said afterwards as he held her close.

"Sex?" she asked, her voice carefully neutral, and he gave a startled laugh.

"Probably not. But I meant... caring for another person. He thought it was a foolish distraction."

"Then I feel sorry for him." She looked up at him, frowning. "The ability to care is what makes us people."

But it also causes pain.

Perhaps she saw the answer on his face, because she sighed and kissed him. They made love again and he finally fell into a troubled sleep. When he woke in the morning she was gone.

. . .

THIS TIME HE KNEW SHE WAS GONE FOR GOOD. IT WAS FOR the best, he told himself. She had her own life and he had his. He needed to focus on winding up this ridiculous will and get back to work. Ignoring the ache in his heart, he put on a suit and went to his office.

"Send for the legal representative," he ordered his secretary as he passed through the outer office.

"Yes, Master Skruj."

Miggs fumbled with the communicator and gave him a desperate look. He shook his head.

"Just tell him to come and see me."

"Yes, Master Skruj."

"Damn puppets," he muttered as he stalked into his office.

For once the financial markets didn't interest him. He didn't even glance at the scrolling stock prices. He kept seeing Bobbi, pale and beautiful in white, walking away from him. Not that she'd actually worn the dress when she left. She'd left it behind, just like she'd left her diamond necklace. Rejecting his gifts just like she'd rejected him.

That's not fair. After all, he hadn't asked her to stay. He had chosen his path long ago, he'd just... hoped he might have company for part of it. *Unlike Towlin,* he thought gloomily. He resolved to put it out of his mind, but he was still staring blindly at the monitor when Miggs timidly announced the Zyran.

"Then send him in," he demanded impatiently.

The legal representative entered and gave him a deep bow.

"Master Skruj."

"I have completed the three tasks."

"Yes, we know."

The Zyran's tail flicked nervously, but he returned Skruj's gaze steadily.

"You had me watched?"

"Of course. Not that we don't trust your word, but we have a duty to our client."

"Your former client," he pointed out, but he couldn't really object. He would have done the same thing.

"And now that you have completed your tasks, I am to give you this."

He gave the envelope the Zyran handed him a suspicious look.

"More conditions?"

"No, the document I referenced. It's just a letter."

"A letter?"

He took it reluctantly.

"Thank you. I will make arrangements to have the remaining shares transferred to you and let you know when it has been completed."

The Zyran bowed and left, leaving him staring at the envelope. He doubted Jakoba had anything to say that he wanted to hear, but it seemed foolish not to read it.

I won't call you friend. We are not friends. We are business partners who have single-mindedly pursued profit to the expense of all else. It was a decision we both chose to make.

But I am dying and it's taking me a long time. It has given me time to think, alone in this room. There is no one here to grieve. There will be no one to mourn me when I am gone.

He shifted uncomfortably, remembering Towlin.

Because I have nothing else to occupy my time, I have been considering you. Unless you change your ways, you will end up dying alone as well. That is why I amended my will—to give you one last chance to change.

The events I have chosen should remind you of who you were, who you have become, and who you might be in the future. Once that knowledge is yours, do with it as you will.

There was no closing signature.

He let the letter fall to the desk as he pulled up a screen and considered his list of assets. Now that he had full control, he could double half of them within a year.

And then what?

Double them again? Hoard them away? Had any of those numbers ever been as satisfying as watching Bobbi radiant and happy in a flame-colored dress? As teaching Tim to skate?

But what if something goes wrong? Fellida had hurt him, but Bobbi could destroy him. And then there was fragile Tim with his uncertain future.

He swore and closed his screens and, for the first time in his life, left the office early. A stunned silence fell as he emerged from his office and he glanced around impatiently. So many employees and he barely knew any of them.

"Go home," he snapped.

"Master Skruj?" Miggs stared at him.

"I said go home. All of you. The offices are closed until after the holidays." Shocked smiles started to appear, and that only irritated him more.

"Oh, thank you, sir—" Miggs began.

"I don't want your thanks. Just see that you return on time."

"Yes, sir."

Miggs had the nerve to grin at him, and he stalked out of the office without responding.

He had forgotten that this was Littima's afternoon off and he had to take a hover cab back to his empty mansion. As soon as he closed the door, silence surrounded him. Silence and darkness. A chill that penetrated his bones. He swore again and went to the control panel, turning up the heat and setting every light in the house ablaze. It didn't help. He was sitting in the middle of the empty living room with all the lights still on when Littima returned.

"Master Skruj?"

"I wish people would stop saying that as if I've lost my mind."

"Yes, sir."

"I may be a fool, but I haven't lost my mind."

"Yes, sir."

His head snapped up.

"Are you calling me a fool, Littima?"

"They were your words, not mine."

His steward placidly returned his stare, and he finally smiled.

"And you are equally a fool for putting up with me."

"Yes, sir." Littima hesitated. "You know when to take a chance in business. Perhaps it is time to extend that knowledge to other areas. Sir."

"I think perhaps you're right."

CHAPTER 16

*B*obbi waited until Eben fell asleep, then quietly rose from the bed. Even in sleep his face was troubled and she longed to comfort him, but she'd only be putting off the inevitable. He so clearly believed what that wretched old male had taught him. And as long as he did, there was no future for the two of them.

This time she'd had the forethought to arrange a change of clothing with Littima. She dressed and silently let herself out of the bedroom. The steward was waiting for her in the kitchen.

"I'm sorry to keep you up so late."

"Not at all, miss. It is my pleasure to drive you home. That is, if you do not feel that you can stay?"

"I'm afraid not. He's not... ready for anything more."

The old male gave her an unreadable look.

"He has changed a lot since he met you."

"I know. But not enough. And he has to decide if he wants to keep going."

Littima sighed.

"I know, but I... hoped."

"I did too."

They looked at each other silently, then Littima rose and drove her home.

She cried herself to sleep that night, and the next night, but during the day she did her best to hide her sorrows from Timmy. He asked about Eben twice, but she managed to put him off. She would tell him the truth after Christmas, she decided. In the meantime there was still a lot to do to get ready. They baked treats and added more decorations and she bought small gifts for all the M'gids, as well as Timmy. His stash of presents was growing daily, but she did her best to keep it under control. As long as she was careful with it, she could use the credits to continue adding small treats to his life for some time to come.

By the time she reported for her last shift before the holiday, she was exhausted but everything was done.

Her coworker Jala was thrilled to be going home for a whole week.

"I love this time of year, don't you? We always do a big bonfire on Last Night and stay up all night drinking hot cider and singing." Jala giggled. "And sneaking off to 'warm up' in one of the bathhouses by the lake. I hope the lake is frozen so we can go skating, but it's probably too early. Do you like to skate?"

The memory of gliding across the ice with Eben's arms around her made her throat tighten, but she managed a nod.

"It's so much fun," the girl continued, happily recounting all of her holiday activities as her fingers flew over the dress she was assembling.

Bobbi listened and nodded and tried not to cry on the clothes. She was concentrating so hard that it took her a moment to realize that Jala had fallen silent. She looked up to see the girl staring down the line. A tall, dark figure was striding towards them, his face grim and determined as he came to a halt in front of her.

"I love you, and I don't want to let you go," he said aggressively. "I want to take you home and make a life with you and Tim and spoil you both senseless and listen to you call me ridiculous names until we're old and grey."

All she could do was stare at him, her mouth open. She didn't even realize she was crying until his face softened and he reached down and gently brushed away a tear.

"Don't cry, sweet. I didn't really think you'd want me too, but I had to—"

"I do," she whispered. "I do want you. I love you too."

"You do?"

They stared at each other for a moment.

"Then kiss her!" someone yelled, and he grinned, the widest, most open smile she'd ever seen on his face, and kissed her.

By the time he raised his head, her knees were threatening to give out. He grinned again, and then he picked her up and carried her out of the factory.

. . .

MUCH LATER THAN NIGHT, BOBBI SNUGGLED AGAINST Eben on the small sofa in her apartment. They had decided to stay there until after the holiday since that was where all the preparations had taken place.

"I can have them transferred to my house if you'd prefer."

"To go with all your other decorations?" she asked dryly.

"I can have the whole house decorated if you wish."

"Next year. There are going to be a lot of changes in Timmy's future so I'd rather ease him into it."

Although she suspected it wouldn't be too difficult. Her brother was already ecstatic about Eben's return.

"About that." He hesitated. "I contacted the teaching hospital. He has a new appointment after the first of the year."

"Really? How did you manage that?"

"A very large donation to their roof fund."

"I'm sure I should say no, but not to this. Thank you."

He shrugged, but she could see that he was pleased.

"So now I finally have you alone," he murmured, his fingers already reaching for the hem of her gown.

"We're not exactly alone."

Timmy was generally a sound sleeper, but she'd been foolish once. She didn't want to take that risk again.

"Come with me."

She took him by the hand and led him into the bedroom.

"That is a very small bed."

"Then we'll have to stay very close."

"An acceptable solution."

He grinned at her and she smiled back.

"Can you be very, very quiet?"

"Yes. Why?" He sucked in a breath as she reached down and freed his erection.

"Very, very quiet," she reminded him as she pushed him gently down on the edge of the bed and went to her knees in front of him.

He managed to keep his word but at the expense of her sheets. She shook her head when she saw the damage he'd caused.

"You ripped holes in my sheets."

"I will buy you new ones. Dozens and dozens of new ones," he said, the picture of languid contentment.

She laughed, and then he flipped her on her back.

"And now it is your turn to be very, very quiet," he whispered as he lowered his head.

"This is the best Christmas ever," Tim said, his thin face flushed with excitement.

"You mean the best First Day," Eben teased, but Tim only grinned.

"I don't care what it's called as long as I get all the presents."

"Timmy," Bobbi scolded as she brought in yet another tray of treats from the kitchen area.

He'd never eaten so many strange things but he had to admit they were delicious. But then again, food had been little more than fuel for his body until now.

"Can I go show Kadra my scooter, sis?"

"All right, but you'd better not even think of leaving this house —even if it's just to 'show' him—without a helmet on."

"I won't," the boy promised, and disappeared down the stairs.

He smiled and shook his head.

"He's very energetic today."

"Yes." She sat down on the couch next to him, a worried look on her face. "I'm afraid it will take a toll on him but I don't want to ruin his Christmas. Do you really think the teaching hospital will be able to help him?"

"If they can't, then we will look elsewhere." He cupped her cheek and raised her face to his. "We will never stop looking."

Tears shimmered in her beautiful eyes.

"Thank you."

"You know, one of the first things Towlin taught me was to set high goals. Goals to aspire towards. But those goals were always monetary, and as soon as I achieved them, I wanted more. I would never have stopped desiring more—and never stopped to appreciate what I had."

She nodded, her face warm and sympathetic.

"I only have one goal now. I want you and Tim to be happy—and every day that I can make that happen will be a success."

"You're going to make me cry," she muttered.

"Then it will be my pleasure to comfort you."

He bent down to kiss her when there was an excited cry from outside. She sighed and went to the window.

"He'd better have that helmet on—Oh. Oh, Eben, come look."

He joined her, sliding his arms around her from behind as they gazed out into the street. It was snowing, white beginning to cover the ground as even more snowflakes floated lazily down from the sky. Below them, Tim and Kadra were already trying to make snowballs, laughing with excitement.

"Timmy was right," she said softly. "This is a perfect Christmas."

Every Christmas would be perfect from now on. He would make sure of it.

He pulled her closer, and together they watched the snow fall.

EPILOGUE

 *ive years later...*

"Pop! Pop!" Tim yelled as he raced into Eben's no longer sterile office, and Eben smiled.

He still didn't quite understand what the explosive sound had to do with fatherhood, but if his son wanted to use it, he wasn't going to object.

"Guess what?"

"What?" he asked solemnly, and Tim laughed.

He was still smaller than most of the boys his age, but the experimental treatments had worked and he glowed with health.

"They're opening the skating rink tomorrow. Can we go? I bet Eva would enjoy it."

"I think she's a little too young for skating, but as long as your sister doesn't think it's too cold, we can all go."

"Aww, you know you're going to get one of those huts with a fireplace. It won't be cold at all."

"As long as Bobbi agrees," he repeated. "And don't start hounding her about it. You know this is a busy time for her."

Those big green eyes gave him a suspiciously innocent look.

"Of course not."

"That includes also mentioning, asking, hinting, and guessing."

"I won't."

He didn't miss the calculating look that crossed Tim's face before he grinned and raced off. He knew he'd missed something, but his beautiful wife was more than capable of handling her younger brother. A few minutes later, the door opened and Bobbi walked in, cradling their sleeping daughter against her shoulder.

"I'm supposed to tell you that it was a request," she said, eyes twinkling, and he sighed.

"I knew I forgot one."

"What? The greatest business mind of your generation forgot such an important detail? I'm shocked, snookums."

"You'll be a lot more than shocked tonight if you keep that up," he growled.

She grinned and came around the desk to settle in his lap. He put his arms around her and nuzzled her neck as he looked down at their sleeping daughter. The combination of their genes meant she had golden skin with only the faintest trace of black markings and a mop of golden curls.

"She's so beautiful," he murmured.

"Yes, she is. Although we might be prejudiced."

"Not at all. I have very high standards."

She laughed and snuggled closer, yawning.

"You look tired, sweet."

"Maybe a little. The show was a lot of work."

He did his best not to react, but she knew him too well and she poked him in the ribs.

"And don't say I told you so."

"I didn't."

She poked him again. "You were thinking it. And anyway, it was a great success. Our principal investor will be very pleased."

"Your principal investor is already very pleased."

He nibbled on the sensitive curve of her neck and she shivered, her nipples peaking. That was dividend enough for him. A year after they were married, Bobbi had presented him with a business plan to establish a small boutique clothing line with Martella. As long as it made her happy, he would have funded it forever, but they had insisted on a formal loan agreement, and somewhat to his surprise, they had made every repayment. The combination of Bobbi's discerning eye and Martella's business sense and connections had proven extremely successful.

And then she'd come to him and said she wanted a child. He'd been thrilled—and terrified. What experience did he have with a loving family? Admittedly he had taken on a father's role for Tim, but the boy was much older. A baby would be so helpless, so dependent on him. She let him think about it for a few days, then sent Tim to stay with the M'gids for two nights and spent that time reminding him how much she loved him and convincing him he would be a wonderful father. Eva was born nine months later.

Fatherhood had proven to be as terrifying as he had imagined, but even more wonderful. He loved watching their daughter grow and change every day while at the same time feeling that time was moving much too quickly.

"Guess who was trying to pull herself up on her crib this morning?" Bobbi asked, confirming his fears.

"Isn't she too young for that?"

"She's very precocious—she takes after her father."

He laughed, and she kissed him. As always the taste of her sweetness made his cock stiffen and she gave him a mischievous smile and deliberately wiggled her ass against his erection. Two could play at that game. Carefully avoiding their sleeping daughter, he slid his hand into the open neck of her blouse and tweaked a pretty little nipple. She squeaked and jumped, and he gave her an alarmed look.

"Is something wrong?"

"N-no. Do that again, very gently."

He obeyed, carefully rolling the stiff little nub.

"Ohhh." She arched into his touch as he caught the sweet scent of her arousal.

"You are very sensitive today, my sweet."

"Mmm." She looked up at him, her lips beginning to curve. "Do you remember the last time I was this sensitive? And tired?"

"When you were pregnant with—" He would have swayed if he hadn't already been sitting. "You mean..."

"I think it's a distinct possibility. We agreed not to do anything to prevent it."

"But it's so soon..."

Her smile faded.

"Too soon?"

"Oh, no, never," he said quickly. "Just surprised. I should have remembered that my wife achieves everything she sets out to do."

"And I should have remembered that my husband had very potent sperm," she said dryly, then laughed. "Our family is growing."

"We should celebrate." He brushed his thumb gently across her nipple, loving the way she shivered.

"Yes, and tell Timmy he's going to be a big brother again and decide on a nursery and all the rest. But right now, I just want to be with you."

"I can do that."

He slid his other hand around to cover her stomach and tugged her closer. Once he had counted his credits, now he counted his blessings—and they multiplied every day.

AUTHOR'S NOTE

Thank you so much for reading **Skruj**! It was such a fun challenge twisting this story into a science fiction romance, and I'm delighted with how it turned out! I hope you enjoyed it just as much!

Whether you enjoyed the story or not, it would mean the world to me if you left an honest review on Amazon—reviews are one of the best ways to help other readers find my books!

Thank you all for supporting these books—I couldn't do it without you!

And, as always, a special thanks to my beta team—Janet S, Nancy V, and Kitty S. Your thoughts and comments are incredibly helpful!

If you loved **Skruj,** you'll also love **Krampus and the**

Crone - another sweet and steamy holiday romance - alien style!

Can a horned alien warrior and an isolated woman grant two children their holiday wish for a family?

Ostracized by the village, Jaelle poses as an old witch to eke out a meager living selling herbal remedies. When children start disappearing from the village, she is determined to find an answer to the riddle. She doesn't expect to find a massive, horned alien - one who sees through all her disguises.

Featuring two precocious orphans, a determined heroine, an unexpected hero, and, of course, a very happy ending!

Krampus and the Crone is available on Amazon!

Or for another fun twist on a classic story, check out ***My Fair Alien***!

Can an alien professor decode the language of love?

When Professor Harak H'gin stumbles across Liza, a bedraggled, beautiful human female, he decides to transform her into a true member of Plumarian society.

But when the lines between teacher and student, human and Plumarian, begin to blur, can Harak resist her newly discovered charms? And can Liza give her heart to an alien who only seems to think of her as an experiment?

My Fair Alien is available on Amazon!

To make sure you don't miss out on any new releases, please visit my website and sign up for my newsletter!

www.honeyphillips.com

OTHER TITLES

Cosmic Cinema

My Fair Alien

Skruj

Horned Holidays

Krampus and the Crone

A Gift for Nicholas

A Kiss of Frost

Stranded with an Alien

Sinta - A SciFi Holiday Tail

HOMESTEAD WORLDS

Seven Brides for Seven Alien Brothers

Artek

Benjar

Callum

Drakkar

The Alien Abduction Series

Anna and the Alien

Beth and the Barbarian

Cam and the Conqueror

Deb and the Demon

Ella and the Emperor

Faith and the Fighter

Greta and the Gargoyle

Hanna and the Hitman

Izzie and the Icebeast

Joan and the Juggernaut

Kate and the Kraken

Lily and the Lion

Mary and the Minotaur

Nancy and the Naga

Olivia and the Orc

Pandora and the Prisoner

Quinn and the Queller

Rita and the Raider

Sara and the Spymaster

Tammy and the Traitor

Folsom Planet Blues

Alien Most Wanted: Caged Beast

Alien Most Wanted: Prison Mate

Alien Most Wanted: Mastermind

Alien Most Wanted: Unchained

Treasured by the Alien

Mama and the Alien Warrior

A Son for the Alien Warrior

Daughter of the Alien Warrior

A Family for the Alien Warrior

The Nanny and the Alien Warrior

A Home for the Alien Warrior

A Gift for the Alien Warrior

A Treasure for the Alien Warrior

Three Babies and the Alien Warrior

Sanctuary for the Alien Warrior

Exposed to the Elements

The Naked Alien

The Bare Essentials

A Nude Attitude

The Buff Beast

The Strip Down

The Alien Invasion Series

Alien Selection

Alien Conquest

ABOUT THE AUTHOR

Honey Phillips writes steamy science fiction stories about hot alien warriors and the human women they can't resist. From abductions to invasions, the ride might be rough, but the end always satisfies.

Honey wrote and illustrated her first book at the tender age of five. Her writing has improved since then. Her drawing skills, unfortunately, have not. She loves writing, reading, traveling, cooking, and drinking champagne - not necessarily in that order.

Honey loves to hear from her wonderful readers! You can stalk her at any of the following locations...

www.facebook.com/HoneyPhillipsAuthor
www.bookbub.com/authors/honey-phillips
www.instagram.com/HoneyPhillipsAuthor
www.honeyphillips.com

Made in the USA
Middletown, DE
04 December 2024

66133957R00103